This book is a book of fiction. Names, characters, places, and incidents are either products of the author's imagination or are used fictitiously. Any resemblance to actual events, locales, or persons, living or dead, is entirely coincidental.

Copyright © by Debra E. Blaine, MD

ISBN Paperback: 979-8-9866211-1-1

ISBN Ebook: 979-8-9866211-0-4

Blaine, Debra

Edited by Carolyn Allard and Kemore Brown

Cover Design by Joe Montgomery

TRUTH IN FICTION

Published by Very Indie Press

Melville, NY

www.VeryIndiePress.com

Printed in the United States

BEYOND THE PILLARS OF SALT

DEBRA E. BLAINE, MD

PRAISE FOR DEBRA E. BLAINE, MD

"In this nail-biting, excellently-paced dystopian thriller, readers will eagerly turn the pages to find out if the best and brightest can save themselves and the future of the human race."

—CB Samet, Four-time award-winning author.

"A character-driven ride through a frighteningly possible future. *Beyond the Pillars of Salt* holds enough truth to scare me and enough science fiction to entertain me until the end."

—Isabella Adams, author of the Markos Mystery Series

ALSO BY DEBRA E. BLAINE, MD

Undue Influences

CODE BLUE: The Other End of the Stethoscope

This book is dedicated to my dear friend

Berry Fowler

With immeasurable gratitude for his abiding encouragement and support.
And in acknowledgement of his genuine and generous spirit such as is rarely seen on planet Earth.

CHAPTER 1

Devon slid down behind the large oak tree in the thick, darkening forest, trying to make himself as small as possible. His breath came in huge gulps that he was sure could be heard for miles, and he struggled to calm himself while his oxygen-starved lungs gasped loudly. He glanced at the makeshift cart he was using to drag his unconscious mother into the mountains. It reminded him of an oversized wagon he'd had as a child. She made no sound, but the soft rise and fall of her chest reassured him she was still alive. Barely. She had lost a lot of blood.

Another shot rang out from behind them and Devon jumped, even though this time it was fainter. He could more sense than hear the raucous laughter of the Marauders, drunk on their own chaos, and he said another prayer that they would give up pursuit. The smell of the forest was soothing; the buzz of insects and the thick canopy of trees that surrounded them offered the impression of coverage and safety. He'd had to ditch the SUV to get this far, hoping they would not follow him off-road. It was getting harder to navigate the narrow terrain. When all was said and done, the Marauders were inherently lazy folks and not interested in hacking their way uphill through tangled undergrowth. That was his hope, anyway.

Not twenty-four hours ago, Devon and his parents happened on an abandoned farmhouse and had planned to hole up there, at least for the night. They soon discovered why it was empty—the previous owners had been slain and left to rot behind the house, a treat left for vultures that scattered as Devon wandered out back. Within an hour of their arrival, the Marauders returned, and Devon had to watch while six men murdered his father. They beat him to a pulp, kicking him in the head and chest, pounding his legs with shovels, and shouting "nigger" and "slave," and then they shot him five times for good measure. There was nothing Devon could do to help, just hunker down and stay hidden behind the old barn where he'd gone to check on any remaining livestock. His mother's condition, weakened by a previous bullet in her shoulder, made it impossible for Devon to leave her. He had been closest to her when the Marauders showed up and had pulled her quietly out of sight. He was about to run to his father's aid, but she had grabbed his arm with her good hand and begged him not to go to Dad. She said he'd be throwing his life away.

As soon as the coast was clear, Devon had run back. Dad opened his eyes for a moment, barely able to speak. "Take care of your mother," he whispered. "Find the Safe Place. Keep heading northwest...into the mountains... Find it, they'll have a doctor. Take her there..." He wheezed as he fought a losing battle for his life. "Go now. Go...quickly... before they..." And then he closed his eyes and was gone. There hadn't even been time for proper tears with the sound of dueled out mufflers floating on the horizon.

It was getting chilly as the sun set. Devon looked around the forest floor. There was plenty of kindling, but a fire was out of the question. They were out of food, but he dug in his pack for water and tried to get his mother to drink. She took one sip and shook her head. She pointed to Devon and whispered, "You," then drifted back into unconsciousness. The wound on her shoulder was wrapped in bloody gauze, and Devon wanted to change the dressing, but he had no clean bandages. He and his father had expected to explore that farmhouse and the town and see what supplies might have been left behind until they could find a doctor for her. The Marauders had found them first.

The smell of evergreens, sugar maples, and red cedars was refreshing, and for a moment he could almost imagine he was just on a hike. He thought back eight years to when he was sixteen, and his dad had taken him into these same Catskills to go horseback riding and then they had jet skied on Lake George. The trip was supposed to be his consolation prize for "winning" the Google Science Fair Competition on the national level, which came with a $50,000 award. After the protests that some half-breed kid like himself should never have been allowed to enter, he did not actually receive the prize money or the medal. The award was retracted entirely, and since then, things had gone from bad to worse. The only ones who could enter contests *or* have access to resorts of any kind now were the Marauders and the White

Supremacists, known widely as the Whispies. They were also the new police. They were the *only* police.

Despite the dropping temperature, gnats and mosquitos were everywhere in the twilight, and Devon wished he had some bug spray. How was he supposed to find the Safe Place? Did it even exist? A part of him dismissed it as just a rumor, born of wishful thinking on the part of large segments of the surviving sane population. Dad had described it as a place of peace. A place where the Old Values still held. Where the color of your skin and the language you spoke and the tradition you practiced were not considered to be important. Only: Could you be honest? Would you be kind? Were you willing to work and contribute whatever skills you had?

Devon vaguely remembered that the United States used to profess these same principles. Before fair elections became impossible and always under question and the despots had moved into the White House. President Ganaffe, who had lost his second term in 2020, took back power four years later, and the Ganaffe clan had held it since. No one saw Ganaffe himself anymore, who would be in his late eighties by now, but someone was holding the reins of power in his name. And pure anarchy had ruled for the last five years.

Devon checked his pocket compass again as he stood up and brushed off his blue jeans. He wondered again how Dad knew in which direction to find the Safe Place, and why he trusted it to be more than a fantasy. But his parents had been privy to a lot of secrets of the resistance, secrets they had not shared with Devon. Better that way, he supposed, in case he'd been captured.

It was a little late to matter, but in the dying light, he surveyed the area for poison ivy; they had been lucky. He gulped down a third of the bottle of water, wanting to conserve it, but he was so thirsty. Mom still lay on the over-sized wagon on top of their packs, which were filled with whatever Devon had been able to retrieve quickly from the SUV before he had sent it careening off a bluff, hoping the Marauders would assume they'd crashed. It had been a moment of impulse to take the cart with him when he left the farmhouse, but he never imagined how heavy it would be to drag it uphill with his mother *and* their belongings in it. Turning wearily, he started back up the mountain, a little more slowly this time, before he had to stop short.

Not ten yards away, a six-foot-tall black bear stood up on its hind legs, facing them and blocking their path.

CHAPTER 2

ussell Vaderman sat at his desk in his office, which was carved into the side of the mountain. His one window overlooked the valley, beautifully surrounded by thick green foliage covering steep slopes and a waterfall to the north. The waterfall was a soothing balm to the tortured souls living in the enclave, and it also supplied their backup generators, but most of the community's power came from solar panels that were installed unobtrusively into the rock. Even if you knew what you were looking for, they were hard to see from above.

The majority of the dwelling spaces were embedded deep within the mountain itself, and the center of the huge canyon had been converted to farmland for grains and vegetables. Peach and apple trees mixed with the edges of the forest. An underground bunker was fully stocked and solid enough to withstand a nuclear blast, so the capriciously shifting weather patterns were not much of a worry either; Russell's only serious concern was earthquakes. The Earth had changed so much in the last few decades. The shifting tectonic plates meant that ground stability was not a given anymore, even here on the East Coast. Of highest priority, they needed to protect the construction project they sheltered from view. It was actually sitting on shock absorbers, so precious was the venture they were working on. But only a few even knew about it as of yet.

Russell looked up a second before he heard the knock on his door. He could always feel the presence of his sister.

Braelyn Plessman came in before he answered, as if she knew his response before he gave it. She had grown so much in the past twelve years, since she had finally learned to understand and harmonize with the unbound potential that had been foisted upon her so long ago in the Northern Peruvian Andes.

"Russ, someone's in trouble. I feel it," she said.

Russell chuckled. "A *lot* of people are in trouble these days, Brae. Is it someone specific?"

Braelyn scowled. "Duh? Yes. Someone whose essence I don't recognize. Someone close by. Someone is lost."

Russell regarded her carefully. Both his sister and he had been subjected to a mind-altering drug when they were tiny children; Russell had been three and Braelyn was seven. It had affected them each differently, but twelve years ago, Russell's mental abilities had been awakened beyond just his high intellect, and he was then able to help Braelyn order her mind to navigate her own mental activity. Before then, Russell was always the rational, capable one, brilliant, with an IQ of 182, although that had come at an enormous price in his childhood. Braelyn had reacted quite differently, always the social misfit and driven to self-destructive behavior as she fled the demons of her mind. But now Braelyn had better control, and her more emotional nature put a powerful spin on her ability. It finally served her instead of ruling her. It had not changed her basic personality, though. Braelyn had always been snarky and obstinate.

"What do you want to do?" Russell asked.

"I *have* to follow it. I have to go…*out.*"

Russell stiffened. "It's not safe, Brae. Not for you, not for the compound. And we are already over the limit of who we can accommodate. And if anyone sees…"

"Russ, we haven't taken in any new people in ages, and there are so many out there suffering. I mean, I know we can't save the whole world, but we can't ignore the whole world either. One more won't make a difference. I'm going. I completed my scouting and firearms training, and I'm taking a semiautomatic. Don't try to stop me."

Russell gave up. There was no changing her mind when his sister was determined. "Take Amira with you at least? And the pups!"

Braelyn exhaled forcibly to show her exasperation. "Sure. Whatever." She stormed out of the office.

Russell looked back at his desk and the equations in front of him. They had two physicists, but they really needed someone well versed specifically in astrophysics and relativity theory. They had so many skilled people, including a few doctors, a contractor, a plumber, two electricians, a meteorologist, a geologist, and more, even a psychiatrist. And a couple of computer-savvy people with extraordinary hacking abilities. But from what Russell understood about the violent changes taking place in the climate and their effect on the

Earth, some sort of escape route was becoming less of a fantasy and more of a necessity. Hence their "construction project."

Several billionaires had built ships and gone into space. Originally it was a lark, more to be a kind of space tourist than anything else, birthed from having so much money they didn't know what else to do with it. But a couple hadn't come back—by design. What had they found out there? Was that the only way to survive now? And how had they managed the energy and time requirements to get anywhere?

More importantly, was there any appropriate place *reachable* that would not put them down with the same despots they needed to get away from? If Russell was thinking this way, surely those in power had already considered it as well.

He put his head in his hands and allowed himself a rare moment of pure emotion. The Earth he loved was violently reclaiming itself; the democracy he used to believe in was gone forever. It was a miracle they had been able to sustain themselves in secrecy in the compound all these years.

Since Ganaffe's denial of election results in 2020, no election in the country had been uncontested, unless it went the way of the GGP—the Great Ganaffe Party. The United States had become a true banana republic, with election guards whose job it was to ensure that everyone voted as directed and congressmen who used intimidation to control what was left of the judicial branch. Freedom of speech was a thing of the past, and nearly all internet activity was censored. When the liberal party fought back, it became an all-out civil war.

Since their dwelling's inception, Russell had not seen the strange visitors who had set him up here in what was once just his getaway home in the mountains. Neither the shaman from his childhood, who had drugged him and irreversibly changed his brain chemistry, nor the mysterious man named Harris, a.k.a. Horatius Marsden, who had somehow yanked him from the hands of the NSA, the Department of Defense, and the NYPD, had shown themselves. Harris had saved Russell's life and instructed him to create this place for the "people of good will" and then simply disappeared.

Russell looked back over the plans on his desk. For twenty years, he'd had a hugely successful career as an architect, and he enjoyed designing large structures. Bridges, buildings, towers—now ships. Anything that he could prepare for durability, functionality, and splendor. But he had no idea how to create enough energy to make a starship functional. His creations had never been meant to go anywhere—quite the contrary. They were designed for stability.

The compound's two resident physicists had looked into various energy sources. Their first thought had been standard nuclear fission reactors, but that was quickly dismissed. It ran the risk that if there were an explosion within the reactor, it would use up all their energy in one burst, and there would be no ability to abort the mission or change course. Next, nuclear fusion was considered, but that still required temperatures of 100M°C. And even if attainable, it would likely not propel them anywhere at light speed, so they'd be stuck in this solar system, where their options were limited.

But there had to be a way; it was like Russell felt the answer hovering out there. A solution he could feel but could not quite see.

CHAPTER 3

Braelyn walked out onto the canyon floor and settled the pack on her back, then hoisted the firearm over her shoulder. At sixty, she was still reasonably strong and fit, partly owing to the bodybuilding she had taken up when they landed in the mountain compound, and partly due to some weird rejuvenating quality that seemed to come along with the effects of the powerful concoction the ancient shaman had inflicted on her at the age of seven. Her special endowment.

In truth, given the massive amounts of other chemicals she had subjected her body to over the years, she had never developed the debilitations that would have been typical for a normal human who'd spent decades addicted to alcohol and cocaine. No cirrhosis of the liver, no cardiac disease, no neuropathy. Of course, doctors had just chalked it up to good genes. But for all that, Braelyn did not think she looked nearly as good as Russell, who appeared to have stopped aging altogether twelve years ago. Except for his eyes. They seemed to see deeper and farther with every passing year. And with more weariness.

Amira Zariz glanced up from adjusting her own gear and gave her a questioning look. Braelyn nodded back and called to the wolves to join them as they turned into the tunnel that led out of the hidden canyon. The "pups," as Russell called them, were faithful and perfectly trained, a male and a female, in the hope that they would mate one day. Russell prided himself on being able to communicate with them, but Braelyn had the real talent. She could connect with them with just a thought, it seemed. She rubbed her fingers deep into their fur, one on either side of her, and they each gave her a brief sniff in acknowledgment.

Braelyn did not know why she didn't like Amira, who was appropriately deferential, even to the wolves, although Braelyn couldn't help but think the respect was just a show. Maybe because it seemed like Amira was, and always would be, her own person, not prone to outside influence, and Braelyn felt she had met her match if it ever came to a battle of wills. At twenty-six, the girl was quick, strong, and sharp, and she had a plethora of useful skills and experience. She had been in the States on vacation when all private air transportation had shut down a few years ago, or so Amira said. Many Americans had fled to Europe, Canada, and Australia when the completely inhuman practices became the norm: shootings, beheadings, torture, and rape on a mass scale. There was no longer any attempt to cover up injustice, and all civilian flights in and out of the country were canceled four years ago.

Amira had been Mossad, though, and Braelyn doubted the Israelis would leave one of their young, capable operatives stranded like that. But if Amira was adept at anything, it was at keeping secrets. If she was in contact with her home base, no one knew about it. Not even Russell. And the wolves seemed to like her well enough, which was a huge endorsement, so Braelyn tried to be positive.

As soon as they entered the tunnel, they all instinctively reverted to stealth, even the wolves, Kobe and Kali; their training was superb. It was imperative that no one hear them approaching. No one could know there was an outlet here. There were silent alarms but no regular guards. This was not the main exit; it was only wide enough for a couple of people to walk side by side, but all the gateways were shrouded in camouflage. They wound their way through the rock in single file. Kobe and Kali first, then Braelyn, and Amira bringing up the rear, with only their flashlights and the noses of the wolves by which to navigate, careful not to kick any rocks and breathing as quietly as they could. It was about three hundred yards to the exit.

In the dim light, Braelyn finally saw the barrier rocks that created a false dead end that worked in either direction just as the wolves came up short. Kali sniffed her hand as if to tell her they had arrived. Both wolves' ears were standing straight up as Braelyn felt below the ledge for the switch. An infrared camera flashed on, and they squatted together to evaluate what life was out and about on the other side. A few birds, a squirrel, but nothing else moved. The dual cameras, hidden in the rock, employed wide-angle lenses, and they could see 180 degrees from the tunnel door.

Silently, they opened the door, which was really a large

face of rock on a hidden hinge. They slipped out and closed the door, and Braelyn felt the latch click softly. Unless someone knew exactly what to look for, it could not be found from the outside. The four of them squatted down to take in the dusk.

"Which direction?" Amira asked in a barely audible whisper.

Instead of answering, Braelyn closed her eyes. She sank into herself to that quiet place she had learned to access. It was full of all sorts of information once she had learned how to look. She had spent the first nearly fifty years of her life fleeing from the chaos of this quagmire of data that seemed to foretell the emptiness of her soul, petrified that it held only the abyss of despair. She had run from one self-destructive relationship to another and had buried herself in alcohol and drugs, desperately trying to escape the Void. All a result of some potion an ancient medicine man stuck in her nostrils half a century ago.

When her brother had finally shown her how to disentangle her emotions from her thinking process, and how to separate the morass of thoughts so that she could understand them, she came to recognize that it was simply her fear of her exceptional cognitive ability that caused the panic. She went from being labeled bipolar and schizoid to finding herself to be a powerful, rational human being who could use her intuition in creative ways. A gift, not a wicked anomaly.

As Braelyn huddled on the ground with Kali standing at attention beside her, she let go and purposefully moved her mind into the empty space. She floated there and waited for the voice that had called to her. A minute passed and then another. There. A woman. A dead woman, if they were not quick enough. It was coming from the southeast.

She opened her eyes and, still with that strange "other sight," she *saw* Amira. She was standing now at an angle to Braelyn and scanning the forest. Amira totally accepted this ability of Braelyn's, without doubt or question; accepted it as a skill to be applied and never derided. Braelyn was momentarily stunned by that knowledge, but she shook it off for the sake of her mission. She stood up slowly.

"She is there," Braelyn pointed. "She is in dire need of help, and I think she is being pursued."

"What is it about her that calls you?" Amira asked, as if this were a commonplace activity. "Is it merely that she is suffering?"

"I feel we need her as much as she needs us, maybe more. And another thing… I don't think she's alone."

They started purposely but silently down the mountain. Kali beside Braelyn and a nose length ahead, while Kobe matched Amira. They made their way through thick trees, deliberately avoiding wider paths, and kept their flashlights off, moving only by the light of the rising moon.

About a mile down the mountainside, Amira raised her hand and they all stopped. Crickets chirped and a few insects buzzed. Braelyn wanted to continue, but Amira held her hand higher. Finally, Kobe gave a quiet, low-throated growl.

They heard the distinct sound then but could not find it. Like a rhythmic snicker on the forest floor. Only Kobe had seen it and crouched down, looking like he might pounce.

"No, Kobe! Step *back*," Amira said firmly in a whisper. Kobe moved back a step with his lips curled, and they walked slowly around, giving the rattler a wide berth.

"Good ear," Braelyn whispered. "I totally missed that."

Amira nodded but did not relax. Braelyn thought if Amira could raise her own ears straight up, that's where they'd be.

Neither did Kobe slacken his jaw. He crouched again and gave a sharp warning bark, and Kali came up beside him. The two wolves stood in front of the women, forming a protective barrier, as a black bear raised itself up on its hind legs to look them over.

Braelyn settled into herself and *reached* for the bear. Sensitivity to animals was one of the first skills Braelyn had delightedly learned she had. Animals were authentic and easy to connect with. Not like humans, who often shrouded themselves with layers of lies and deception.

We mean you no harm. We are not like the others.

She sent the thought as an image to the animal, whose fear and agitation she was sensing. The five of them faced off in silence for a full minute. Then the bear lowered itself, turned, and shuffled away. Amira looked at Braelyn questioningly.

"The Marauders think it's great fun to shoot and torture bears," Braelyn said. "Actually, bears, coyotes, foxes … anything they find. They think it makes them look tough. So now wild animals that never used to bother much with humans have learned to see us as a threat, and they will attack at the slightest provocation."

Amira grunted. "Humanity no longer fits in on this planet. You know, in my tradition, humans were originally meant to be custodians of the Earth, not conquerors. In our quest for domination, we have destroyed the very land that sustains us."

"Speaking of which," Braelyn said, holding up her

hands as the first drops of rain began to fall. The forest became darker, and she looked up and noticed the moon was suddenly gone. "I hope this won't be another tropical storm. They're getting more frequent and more violent lately."

"How far to the 'voice' you heard?" Amira asked.

"Not far, I think. It was moving toward us, but now it stopped. Another few hundred feet."

———

Too late, Russell checked the weather satellite. *Damn*, why didn't he look before the team went out into the forest? The little bit of rain that had been heading to them a few hours ago had abruptly escalated, and the wind pattern showed whorls on the radar that could make for gusts reaching 80 mph already, and it had barely made landfall. Used to be, the mountains stopped the storms from doing too much damage, but that had changed of late, and Braelyn and her little crew were heading southeast *down* the mountain, which would leave them more greatly exposed. He pressed the yellow alert to initiate a routine tie-down for the compound; it would also advise everyone there was a storm coming and to stay within the mountain.

On cue, Ricardo knocked and came in; he had been anticipating the alert.

"Hey, Ric, what's our status?"

"We're in good shape," Ricardo answered. "We have most of the crop already bundled and in storage, since it's Friday, and it's already our day to stash the week's take. A few tractors are parked by the side of the mountain, and Joshua is out there tethering them; although, I doubt the winds will be high enough to move a two-ton tractor."

"Good," Russell said. "Stand ready to initiate retraction of the solar panels if this becomes a hurricane and the gusts go over 75 mph. These storms are getting way too frequent and violent."

CHAPTER 4

Arnold Higgins walked into the White House with some trepidation. He wanted this job and had competed fiercely for this interview. No one had actually seen President Martine Ganaffe in years, but he *was* the president, so Arnold was not surprised when he was summoned to the Oval Office for this meeting. Why was his stomach in such knots?

He was greeted by a capitol officer and strip searched before being escorted upstairs, where he was instructed to wait in a room for his evaluation; it was not the Oval Office, and that made him more nervous. He was invited to have some tea that had been placed on a small table off to the side, and after pacing around for a bit, he poured himself a cup. It had a strong, unidentifiable taste, curious but not unpleasant. Arnold noted the cameras on the ceiling at every corner, surveying the entire room. He took a seat and finished the tea, then sat tapping his foot quietly. More to let out stress than out of impatience. Finally the door opened, after at least twenty minutes.

Justine Ganaffe walked in accompanied by her entourage. Her perfume was heavy enough to nearly make Arnold cough, and her dress was tight-fitting and off the shoulder, displaying her perfectly sculpted body. A body that had surely been through several plastic surgeries at the age of fifty-two to make her look like a woman in her early thirties. Beneath her makeup, there were still some lines and pockmarks that came from stress and unsuccessful pharmaceutical interventions. Still, she walked smoothly and gracefully, in stark contrast to the three men who accompanied her with semiautomatic sidearms strapped to their belts, all of whom looked a bit like zombies stiffly marching along. They took positions around the room but never took their eyes off Arnold. In addition to Justine Ganaffe and her armed cronies were two men who flanked her and appeared more relaxed. Arnold was sure they were also armed, but their guns were not in plain sight.

Arnold stood up and bowed to her as he had been instructed to do. He waited for her to extend her hand and then he took it tenderly in his own and bent his face over it to kiss her ring. A three-carat ruby sat adjacent to an even larger diamond, and Arnold's eyes nearly popped looking at it up close. He lifted his head and waited for her to nod to him before standing up straight again.

The men who appeared more human escorted her to a plush armchair and stood at each side once she sat down. She then nodded to Arnold again and he returned to his seat. The guards with the weapons were disturbing. Not because they were armed but because they seemed completely vacuous.

Like there was no one home behind their eyes. Arnold shivered and tried to focus on Justine and her consorts.

"So," Justine began, "you think you would be up to the job of Chief of Staff to President Ganaffe." She wasn't asking a question; she seemed to be more demanding a justification for his hubris.

Arnold swallowed. He had been prompted for this part as well. "I am a faithful follower of the Great Ganaffe Party and am well-versed in all accepted models of persuasion. My goals are President Ganaffe's goals; where he leads, I will pave the way. I have managed press releases and media transfigurations and have evaluated staff for loyalty throughout the judicial sector." Arnold couldn't help but feel like his speech sounded scripted. Hardly avoidable, he supposed, since it was. But monotone was an accepted, perhaps even expected, pattern of discourse. He held his breath and thought his face must look as stony as the zombielike guards around the room.

The silence stretched out. Justine stood up and walked over to him. She sat on the arm of his chair and stroked his neck. *This* he had not been prepared for. Arnold stared straight ahead and tried to keep his hands from trembling, unsure what was expected of him.

"Do you find me attractive, Mr. Higgins?"

Arnold's mouth was dry. He nodded. "Yes, ma'am. I do."

"And if I find *you* attractive, will that be a problem for you?"

"No, ma'am. I am at your service in any way you choose," Arnold answered.

He was completely confused and fought to keep that from showing on his face. He had always thought of himself as somewhat average in the looks department. He was carrying an extra ten pounds and did not exercise much, and he wasn't an exceptionally stylish dresser. Was Justine testing him, or was this going to be part of his job description? He wasn't sure how he felt about that. Her perfume was thick, and he felt giddy with it, and the room seemed to spin and swell. Arnold sunk into himself and slowed his breathing while keeping his eyes alert but averted toward the floor.

Finally, Justine nodded and stood up. She managed to brush his inner thigh as she lifted herself from the arm of the chair. As she walked toward the door, she flicked her long blonde hair out behind her, and the stone-faced guards moved to follow her. She looked over her shoulder, and with a mischievous, "He'll do," she was gone.

Arnold sat as stiff as a board in the chair. The two consorts who had flanked her had barely controlled snickers on their faces. One of them reached out his hand. "I'm John Sentics. Welcome aboard."

Arnold was incredulous. "That's it? I thought I needed to be interviewed by President Ganaffe?"

The other consort shook his head. "No one sees President Ganaffe." He reached out his hand as well. "Brian Wordsmyth. Pleased to meet you. We'll get you set up in your new residence. From this day forward, your life is within these walls. You do not leave until you're dead."

Arnold swallowed and shook each of their hands. *Step one.*

CHAPTER 5

Devon stared at the bear, his heart pounding. Dear God, help us! he prayed silently. He desperately tried to remember what he had learned about bears. He knew that brown bears and black bears called for completely different defense maneuvers. He also knew you were never supposed to run from a bear—not that he could with his mother in a cart. For one breed of bear, it was better to make yourself small and nonthreatening, and for the other, it was advised to stand tall, make a lot of noise, and try to scare them off, but in his panic, he couldn't remember which was which. Why hadn't he researched this, knowing they would be going into the mountains? He knew brown bears were intrinsically more aggressive, but this was black bear country. He'd also heard that bears were being hunted and tortured, so all bets could be off.

He straightened up slowly, afraid to meet the bear's eyes but wishing he could talk to it. They had the same enemy, after all. Rain suddenly started pelting down on the three of them, and even the bear appeared momentarily distracted by it. Devon looked at his mother, who was soon to be soaked, and what then? Pneumonia? He anxiously wanted to pull out a tarp to cover her, but he couldn't take his eyes off the bear.

Just when he thought he might break down completely, there was a rustling in the bushes off to the side, and both Devon and the bear turned to it instinctively. Two women and two wolves appeared out of the falling darkness. Devon didn't know if they were friend or foe and wondered if his mother would tell him—if she could—to use this moment to flee and save himself. But he stood frozen and staring.

The women seemed to size up the situation immediately, and strangely, neither seemed surprised to see Devon or the bear. The older one put her hand out at waist level, palm down, and approached the bear slowly, her gaze fastened on the animal's eyes. Devon wanted to scream at her not to provoke it, but he found he had no voice. She stopped about six feet from it, and no one spoke.

After an eternity, the bear snorted, relaxed its posture, and shuffled away into the shadows.

The younger woman came over to Devon, a wolf at her side. Suddenly, the flight, the hunger and fear, the shock, and the exhaustion took over, and Devon sunk to his knees on the ground. This put his face level with the wolf's face, and he was sure his life was over, but the woman squatted down beside them and stroked the wolf until it sat down, too, now looking more like a friendly dog. She asked Devon his name, and he was barely able to answer.

"My name is Devon Simmons. Please help my mother. She

was shot two days ago, and it's been too long; she's dying." Tears welled up and started streaming down his face.

The younger woman went to his mother and checked the pulse at her neck. "She's still with us. My name is Amira and this is Braelyn. Come, we will help you with the cart. Clever that you brought it. How did you get all the way up here on foot like this?"

But Devon couldn't answer. All his energy was being spent in his struggle to continue up the mountain. He didn't even know where they were taking him, but they seemed kind, and he could not go on alone anymore.

It seemed to take the little crew forever to climb up the sloping mountain, dragging the cart with an unconscious woman on it with them, and by then, the sky had opened up completely. No one asked what else was in the cart, and there was no chance to sort through it anyway. Devon had pulled out a tarp and covered his mother, but they were all drenched in no time. The wet fur made the wolves look pathetic, but they maintained their disciplined escort and abruptly pulled up short just before they reached a part of the mountain that jutted upward at an angle Devon knew he could not climb. Both animals growled in unison.

Amira turned immediately. A lone figure in a light jacket stood soaked, with no pack or supplies, looking bedraggled. It could have been a man or a woman, more muscled than most women but smaller and slighter than most men. Smooth, dark brown, shoulder-length hair was tied back, and the hands looked both delicate and strong. The stranger stood about twenty feet from the mountainside, as if searching for a way through the rock, and stiffened when the wolves came into view but relaxed for a minute at the sight of the women.

"Who are you?" Amira demanded.

The figure looked uncertain. "My name is Sahina Keter. I was looking for shelter. The storm took me by surprise. Do you know someplace to get out of the rain?" The figure glanced at the makeshift cart with Devon's mother lying on top and a tarp thrown over all but her head and then peered at Devon, who was now leaning against it. Devon was breathing heavily and barely awake, but he watched the interaction and hoped it would be short so that they could get to someplace dry. The rain was steady and merciless.

"Do you need help? I can help you with them," Sahina said.

Braelyn walked up to the strange individual and peered through the dark downpour. "Why would you help us? What do you want?"

"I told you, I just want to get out of the rain." Sahina nodded at Devon and his unconscious cargo. "It looks like they do too. Can I help?" Devon had the uncanny feeling that the rain wasn't actually bothering this guy, despite his stated interest in getting out of it.

Braelyn appeared to sense something odd about him as well, although she seemed inclined to take the stranger along, but Amira stepped between them. It was an awkward moment, as if it was the first time she had ever overridden Braelyn on anything, and Braelyn looked angry. But Amira was impervious to her companion's defiance and walked up to stand within six inches of Sahina; she said nothing but searched the newcomer's eyes for a full minute. Then she turned to Braelyn and shook her head ever so slightly.

Braelyn bristled with anger. "Who are you to say the outsider shouldn't come in? This is *my* compound, mine and

Russell's," she said in a loud whisper, glaring at Amira before she pushed past her and addressed the stranger.

"Come with us, Mr.—uh—Ms. Keter."

Amira grabbed Braelyn's shoulder, her face a vision of alarm. "Wait," she whispered.

"Not your place," Devon heard Braelyn say to Amira. Sahina was also watching the interplay between the women. He almost looked amused.

"I'm an engineer," Sahina said. "It sounds like you have friends somewhere… I could be useful."

That seemed to clinch it for both Braelyn and Amira, each in opposite ways. Braelyn obviously wanted to bring Sahina along, and Amira seemed more determined to send him away. Amira dragged Braelyn a few steps away from the intruder and closer to Devon.

"Braelyn, why would he say that? What does he know about us? What would your brother say?" Amira's voice was low and urgent.

"My brother…" Braelyn looked livid, but she controlled herself. She spoke slowly and deliberately. "Russell didn't want me to come out at all, for *any* survivors. But my brother knows I am capable of making some decisions too."

Devon quailed at the argument. He felt like he could barely stand up any longer. Thunder crackled suddenly overhead, sounding like it was nearly on top of them. Seeing his discomfort, Sahina strode over to Devon in three swift steps, which appeared more like gliding than walking, and put an arm under him for support. Devon leaned on the stranger in relief and found him to be much stronger than Devon would have guessed, but the deed prompted the larger wolf to bound over and stand in front of them. It bared its teeth and growled, blocking the way.

The darkness was interrupted by more flashes of lightning, sporadically revealing the grim shadow of the huge canine. Devon felt frozen; the last thing he wanted to do was to provoke the animal, but he could not stand there much longer, Sahina's arm or not. The wolf stood nearly four feet tall, despite its heavy coat being drenched and lying flat on its back; with ears upright and tilted forward, lips curled back, and looking nothing less than terrifying. The smaller animal, however, seemed to be weighing in on Braelyn's reaction, but ultimately came to stand beside its fellow wolf. Which meant Devon was staring straight at them both.

A flicker of doubt passed across Braelyn's face, but the longer they stood out there, the worse the chances were for Devon's mother, who needed medical attention as soon as possible. Devon decided they must be very near their destination so that they couldn't tell this wanderer to go away and then continue on unseen. Maybe it was better to bring the drifter in and keep him from reporting back to whoever might have sent him. Devon just prayed they'd hurry up and make a decision.

The forest was shattered again by lightning and the sound of thunder, followed by a tree splitting and falling onto the forest floor not thirty feet away from them.

That was the deciding factor for Braelyn. "Kobe," she called, and the larger wolf reluctantly backed down. The other wolf sniffed at Sahina for a second and went to stand beside its mistresses. Braelyn motioned to Amira to pick up the cart handle, and Sahina shifted his arm under Devon to assist him. Braelyn nodded and walked up to the side of the mountain and slipped her fingers into a ridge in the rock. It had no outstanding features and blended right into the mountainside, but a small digital lock popped out silently, and Braelyn punched in an access code.

———

When Devon woke up, he was in a bed in what looked like a hospital or clinic. He was warm and dry, and he vaguely remembered being rescued from a bear by two women and two wolves, and there was something about a strange person who helped him the last few steps, but most of it was a blur. His mother was nowhere to be found, but there was an attendant at the far end of the room.

"Hello?" Devon said, but he could barely speak up and wasn't heard. The attendant walked out, and Devon managed to sit up and look around. There was a tray of food next to his bed, and after determining that he was definitely alone, he dug into it. He couldn't even have said for sure what it was, only that it was tasty. Some kind of grain and fruit porridge and a slice of fresh-baked whole grain bread. He gulped the water next to it as well.

He stood up gingerly just as a woman walked into the room.

"Hey, hey, slow down," she said. "You've been out for a while. Is your name Devon?"

Devon nodded. "Where's my mother? She was with me. Who are you? Where am I?"

"Easy there. My name is Dr. Lister. Your mom—that's the woman you were with? She is recovering. She had a bullet lodged in her shoulder and had lost a lot of blood, and she was also becoming septic. She may have sustained some nerve damage, too, but she's out of surgery, on antibiotics, and recovering. I'm sure she'll be thrilled to see *you*! She's not quite completely awake yet. What happened to you two?"

"Please let me see her," Devon said, embarrassed by the tears that were filling his eyes. "Is this... Is this the Safe Place?"

"The what? This is our encampment. It's lucky we got to you guys when we did. The storm hit shortly thereafter. It's a biggie. Winds are near 120 mph."

Devon was puzzled. "I don't hear any wind."

"That's because we're underground," Dr. Lister said. "C'mon, I'll take you to your mom."

Teresa Simmons was lying in a hospital bed in a room that resembled an ICU. She had an IV line in her right arm and a nasal cannula under her nose providing oxygen. A monitor on the wall over her head recorded her blood pressure, heart rate, and oxygen concentrations. There were a bunch of wave patterns showing other bodily functions that Devon did not understand, but her breathing was restful and her color was good. Devon walked over to her bedside and took her hand. She opened her eyes.

"Mom..."

"Devon. My sweet boy. You did it."

"Mom, Dad is dead," he choked out and tears ran down his cheeks. "They butchered him, and all I did was watch!"

Teresa took her son's arm. "That's what your father wanted. Neither of us would have ever forgiven ourselves if you'd thrown your life away, just to say you tried. You could not have made any difference but to die with him."

"But you always taught me to never give up."

"Sometimes wisdom is knowing when to lay low and fight another day."

Devon rested his head on his mom's good shoulder and let his tears fall quiet and hidden. "Is this the Safe Place?" he asked.

"I think so, darling. I think we made it. *You* made it. God bless you." Teresa drifted back off to sleep.

CHAPTER 6

Russell sat in his favorite armchair in his underground office. The winds outside were brutal. They had locked down the solar panels and pulled casings over the windows. They were truly in underground mode. Braelyn sat across from him, sipping tea.

"So, who are they?" Russell asked.

"I don't know. The boy is emotionally vulnerable right now, but I feel he is very intelligent. I didn't exactly get to have a friendly conversation with him. The woman was near death. Another few hours, and I doubt she would have made it. They did have some interesting equipment with them and…plans. Paper stuff, graphs and drawings. Who *does* that these days? Everything should be digital. If it's important, it could have been lost or damaged beyond recovery in the storm."

Russell considered. "Maybe people who are looking to operate *sub rosa*. Anything digital can be hacked. And Brae—

he's hardly a boy. Mid-twenties, I heard, and he watched his family get brutally attacked. No one who has survived in these mountains is a boy any longer. What about the straggler you found sniffing around?"

"Well, he was very secretive about the papers," Braelyn said, ignoring the inquiry about Sahina Keter. Russell guessed she had not figured the guy out yet and so was not ready to discuss her judgment.

She continued, "Devon said they were his mother's and he did not understand them, but I think he was lying. I think he knows exactly what's on those papers and what they mean."

"Why would he do that? Did you bring them up with you?" Russell sighed. He wished Braelyn would tell him about this stranger. Her decision *was* probably appropriate, given that they had been discovered, but they needed to know who he is and what he wants.

Braelyn smirked. "Some of them." She handed them to him and then got up to lean over the back of Russell's chair to peruse the papers along with him. "What do they mean?"

Russell got very quiet. A throwback to his early days when he was sorting through something. The plans were architectural, and Russell understood that part well enough, having designed numerous buildings in his life. For a moment, he thought longingly of his business on Sixth Avenue in New York City, where he had fashioned spectacular structures that could withstand Category 5 hurricane force winds and earthquakes up to 8.0 on the Richter scale, yet were stunningly beautiful. The skill had served him well when they created this encampment. Those were the days of relative peace, the days before…

As he looked at the drafts, they lifted off the page in his mind's eye and turned in three-dimensional space. They were coded, but nevertheless, he read the language under the code, and his breathing increased with his excitement. This was amazing! This was exactly what they needed.

"What is it, Russ? What does it mean?" Braelyn asked.

Russell looked up. "I can't. I can't just…steal this. I need to talk to the woman who wrote these." He gathered the papers and headed down to the hospital wing without any explanation.

———

Braelyn sighed in exasperation. How like her brother not to explain himself! But she hadn't explained herself either. Braelyn thought about Sahina Keter and the puzzle the visitor created in her mind. Funny, sometimes she was sure he was a man and sometimes she was sure she was a woman. Not that Braelyn cared either way, but the ambiguity made her mistrustful. Particularly because, for some bizarre reason, Braelyn just didn't feel like she could ask. Now *that* was odd! Braelyn didn't generally have any trepidation about confronting anyone about anything. But there was something about this individual…

But the impulse she'd had to bring him in was not wrong, she was sure of that. If she hadn't, their cover would have been blown for certain. The compound had not yet had to deal with the scenario of an unwelcome intruder. She wondered what Russell would do if they decided Sahina was dangerous. They couldn't kill someone just like that… *they* didn't do that kind of thing. They were not the GGP. But what were their choices?

Since no one had yet decided what Sahina's status should be, he was in a small, isolated residence in the compound for now, with food, dry clothes, and a bed. There was a guard outside his door to escort him if he needed to go anywhere. Not exactly a prison, but he wasn't allowed to go wandering about on his own.

CHAPTER 7

Arnold Higgins was settling into his new ten-foot-by-ten-foot home. It was essentially an office with a small bookshelf, where he supposed he could put some family pictures, since no one was allowed to read books anymore. He found a computer on his desk, which was bolted into place, and he quickly discovered that it had severely restricted access to the internet. Kind of a waste, since pretty much nothing was posted on the internet anyway without the GGP's approval. There was a half-room divider behind which was a small bed with folded sheets and a blanket tossed on it adjacent to a meager dresser. The bathroom was down the hall. John and Brian had said he would be able to send for clothes and a few personal items, but they would have to be screened before he could have them, so he should be conservative. Anything that was found to be unbecoming of his position would be destroyed.

Arnold looked around the room. This was going to be

home now? He felt the sting of parting from his wife, Hannah, and their four-year-old daughter, Eve, knowing he was probably never going to see them again. His wife had given up begging him to reconsider; his daughter just cried, thankfully too young to really understand. He had told them it was an honor to do this work, which was so needed right now. More than anything, Arnold wanted to be seen as having been on the right side of history. But Hannah had whispered that was entirely dependent on *who* was writing the history, and then she let him go.

There was a knock on the door and John Sentics came in. "Hungry?"

They went down to the dining area, and John studied him while Arnold ate something that passed for a hamburger. It had a strange aftertaste, like the tea. Not unpleasant, just unusual. Arnold wondered why John wasn't eating.

"I take my meals upstairs. You will, too, after you've been here awhile and passed the probationary period. You know, the last chief of staff didn't quite cut it. Very promising in the beginning, but he just didn't have his principles straight, so we're being extra careful."

"What happened to him?"

"Same thing that happens to anyone Justine doesn't approve of." John shrugged. "He 'went away.'

"Your duties will begin tomorrow," John continued. "You'll be formulating the copy material for our next propaganda program. Our community police force needs to be encouraged from time to time. Mostly, they do a great job all on their own, even if they are a little overzealous, but sometimes we do want to keep them focused. We have been looking for what's probably a mythical asylum that some of the resisters are talking about. No one has been able to find it, so it probably doesn't exist, but we do have a number of well-trained patrols out there in addition to the Whispies—who tend to be on the cruder side. These scouts are prepped with specialized infiltration techniques if they happen upon suspicious activity. Have you heard anything about this?"

Arnold frowned. "Nothing specific. Word on the street is, it's in the mountains somewhere; I personally think it's out west. But given what happened to the Rocky's with the last earthquake, I don't think anything could have survived up there. 'Course, they could mean the Sierra Nevada's, but I heard that terrain has been mostly untravellable for a couple of years now, too, so what good would it do anyone if no one can get there? And I can't figure how they would get supplies. Why do we care if they're isolated even from their own people?"

John raised an eyebrow. "President Ganaffe *always* cares if there is anyone or anything that does not support him. He demands one hundred percent allegiance from one hundred percent of the population." John squinted suspiciously at Arnold. "I thought you knew that."

Arnold felt a sweat break out on the back of his neck. "Of course I know that. Just that logistically…well, I didn't know he—we—were able to enforce it."

John continued to eye him warily. "That is what we do," he said, and left the rest of his sentence unspoken.

Arnold changed the subject. "So are we… Are we expected to attend to Justine's, um, womanly needs? Doesn't her husband object?"

"Harrumph," John said. "Murray? He's a pansy ass. Everyone knows it. He contributes nothing but what he is told to contribute. Not even sure he'll be going with the party when—" John stopped abruptly.

"Where is the party going?"

"Never mind. Nothing for you to concern yourself with right now. We're still checking you out. If you pass your initial screenings, which will include a couple of evenings with Justine, I'm sure, then we can talk freely."

"And if I don't pass?"

John chuckled. "Then I guess you'll be 'going away' too."

Arnold passed several of the zombie guards as he went back to his "office" and was mildly alarmed to find that one of them was stationed outside his door, recording all his comings and goings. He guessed that included the bathroom, which was down the hall. The guards creeped him out, all the more because he felt he was supposed to ignore their presence. But he stopped at his doorway and looked at him.

"What's your name?"

The zombie turned slowly to face him. The eyes were empty. "I serve" was all that Arnold got. Then he (it?) turned back to stare straight ahead.

"Where are you from?"

No response. Arnold wanted to shake it and demand an answer, but he sensed a great danger hidden in its silence, and he decided not to rouse it. As he walked inside his office, the zombie turned slowly, and those dead eyes followed him in. A chill went up Arnold's spine.

CHAPTER 8

Russell found himself almost running down to the hospital wing, without regard for what kind of state this woman would be in. He had to force himself to slow down. She might not be up for questioning. She might not even know what she'd been carrying. But he felt such an urgency; they were running out of time here.

Devon was sitting next to his mother, holding her hand and dozing. Although he had escaped being physically injured, the stress, the exhausting trip up the mountain, and the loss of his father had taken a great toll on him. Russell forced himself to slow his breathing as he walked into the small recovery area.

Fortunately, there were not a lot of patients needing this high level of care. They only had three beds in this room, but the area was seldom used. Most medical services were attended to next door and were for an occasional mishap injury, like a broken bone or a laceration. Perhaps that was because sicker individuals couldn't make it into the mountains, or perhaps it was because the compound had clean air and clean water, all the food was organically grown, and there was no access to junk food, tobacco, or even alcohol. There were plenty of baked goods, including chocolate brownies and muffins, but no preservatives or unnecessary chemicals of any kind were in any of their foods. They had no one with diabetes, heart disease, or even high blood pressure. Whether they all started out that way or whether it was from the lack of *ersatz* additives, all the residents of the compound were a hearty bunch. Which was good, since their physiological fortitude was soon to be stretched to the max.

Devon looked up when Russell entered. He stood up and placed himself protectively in front of his mother, who seemed to be in a deep sleep.

Russell sized him up. He was not more than twenty-five, about five feet ten, with a slight build and short black curly hair. His clothes were rumpled, as if he either did not have others or just had not changed them in a week, and he had obviously been through hell. Russell didn't want to make his life more stressful by questioning him so quickly, but life *was* inherently stressful these days.

Russell offered his hand and introduced himself. "I manage this compound. I'm glad we found you when we did; your mother might not have made it much longer. How did you come to be heading into the mountains?"

Devon sat back down in the chair, as if he could barely hold himself up anymore.

"My mother was dying. My father was murdered. Before he died, he told me there was sanctuary somewhere here in the mountains and that I should find it and bring her here. If you hadn't found us, I don't know what... My mother and I are both very grateful to you for saving her life."

Russell pulled a chair over from the next bed and sat down. "Were you being chased for the glee of the game, or were they looking for something specific from you?"

Devon fidgeted and dropped his eyes. He swallowed a couple of times and then looked up at the panel over his mother's head. Heart rate and blood pressure were stable, and her oxygen saturation was 98 percent. He said nothing.

Russell studied him quietly. *He does know what those papers mean.*

Finally, the silence got to be too much, and Devon looked up.

"Is this the Safe Place? I have to know."

"I have never heard us called that specifically," Russell said, "but you are safe here. We are a haven from the GGP, the Whispies, and even the climatic violence the Earth is unleashing these days. And I guess I must also tell you that since it would be devastating if we were discovered, I will want you to stay here so you cannot be compelled to reveal us to anyone who means us harm. We are well defended, but I do not want to have to test those defenses against an all-out assault from the current governing forces."

Devon swallowed again. He rubbed the heels of his hands against his temples for a moment and then nodded. "My mother..." He glanced at the sleeping form on the hospital bed. "My mother is a scientist. She made some...discoveries. The GGP wants them, but she didn't want to give anything to them, so they sent the Whispies to get them. She wiped the drives, drew some of the plans out on paper, and the rest is on a flash drive." Devon hesitated for another minute, then reached into his pocket and pulled out a sealed plastic bag containing a small USB drive unit. "I don't understand all of it. She also insisted we bring a containment module that we all developed together. It can store gamma radiation." His voice dropped to nearly inaudible as he said the last, as if hoping Russell would miss that part.

Russell raised an eyebrow but stayed otherwise steady. Years of practice at not showing emotion while figuring out what was in front of him served him well.

"My mother said…she said the people in the Safe Place would need this. It was really important to both of my parents that we get it here."

"May I see the USB drive?"

Devon quickly stuffed it back in his pocket. "I'd rather you let my mother show it to you, if that's okay. She *is* going to be all right, isn't she?"

Russell smiled. "I believe so, Devon. And I understand your caution. We are very much in need of what it sounds like you might be carrying. I'll come back in a couple of hours. Hopefully, your mother will be awake and able to talk then."

Russell looked at the woman on the hospital bed. She was olive skinned with sharp features and coarse, curly hair that was starting to gray. Thin and muscular, she hadn't been knocked down easily. Even in sleep, her face had a certain tension in it that bespoke sheer determination.

"Do you have everything you need? We prepared a room for you to sleep in, and there's a cafeteria on the next floor when you get hungry. We can give you some clean clothes as well. Your mother will be well cared for here; you needn't worry."

"Thank you. I'd prefer to stay here until she's stronger."

Russell nodded. This kid was as determined as his mother. Nothing but the cold, hard truth would be acceptable to him. They had to win them both over somehow. And quickly.

CHAPTER 9

Teresa Simmons opened her eyes slowly and looked around while keeping her head as still as possible. She was afraid to move, afraid the relative comfort she was feeling would be replaced by the searing pain in her shoulder that had become so much a part of her existence that she had forgotten what it was like when it wasn't there. But nothing hurt. Not much, anyway. She carefully sat up on her right elbow, noting that her left arm was stiff, and her sensation felt blunted down to her fingertips.

She was hooked up to an IV, and an oxygen canula sat below her nose; a pulse oximeter on her right index finger read 99 percent. She managed to adjust the pillow behind her to sit more upright and removed the canula from her face while keeping her eyes on the pulse ox. After a minute, it dropped to 98 precent. She sat up slowly and swung her legs around the side of the hospital bed, letting the pulse ox slip off her finger. A quiet beeping barely registered to her, but a man and a woman appeared at her side within half a minute. The woman nodded to her colleague, and he left the room.

"How long have I been out?" Teresa asked.

"Several days. My name is Dr. Tobi Lister." She nodded toward Teresa's shoulder. "I'm afraid you may have some permanent nerve damage in that arm. The bullet ricocheted into the brachial plexus when it expanded, and…" The doctor shrugged. "You're alive, and you should have *some* use of the arm. More function may return in time, and we can try some rehabilitative therapy. When you're up to it."

Teresa looked up, really seeing the doctor for the first time. She was in her sixties, thin, with gray highlights in what used to be dark-brown hair, and a wise but gentle face. "You saved my life. Thank you." Then she looked around frantically. "I remember my son being here, but…was I dreaming? Is he okay?" Her voice rose in panic.

"Easy there. He's fine. I sent him off to get some sleep. He was falling down on his feet. I promised him you'd be okay." Dr. Lister smiled, and Teresa could just imagine how hard it had been to convince Devon to leave her side.

At that moment, the man from before came back in pushing a cart, and Teresa could smell the steaming soup on it. He helped Teresa move to a chair and set the food tray in front of her. As he left, another man entered the room.

The newcomer was just over six feet, and his hair was dark brown, long and wavy in the front but cropped shorter in the back, and he looked toned and muscular beneath his clothes. He carried himself with an air of authority, although he was dressed very casually in jeans and a dark purple button-down flannel shirt. There was something about him that piqued her interest yet cautioned her at the same time.

He wanted something from her. He'd found her research. Had she rescued it from the tyrants only to have it fall into another's irresponsible hands? How could she know who to trust anymore? She quailed inside.

"Looks like Dr. Lister has worked another miracle," he said and smiled at both women. "My name is Russell Vaderman. I was the instrument through which this compound was founded."

Teresa licked her lips from the tasty soup. "That's an interesting choice of words. You didn't create this place?"

Russell pulled up a chair and nodded to the doctor, who took her cue and left. "At the time, I had no idea such a place would be necessary. That was twelve years ago. 'Forces,' of sorts, conspired to set us up, and we are very grateful for that."

"So this is the Safe Place?"

"We have never called it thus, although it is likely one of the safest places on Earth right now, certainly in this country. You won't find any Whispies or Marauders or members of the GGP here, and anyone who is aggressive to others is dealt with. In truth, we try not to admit anyone who is not of… good character." Russell smiled a little mischievously. "So I hope you have no aspirations of oppressing anyone and, I hope you have no affiliations with what currently passes for government in this country. That would be most unfortunate."

Teresa relaxed a little. But it could also be just words. Anyone can profess an attitude while planning something completely different. In the world she had just come from, deceit dripped from everywhere.

Russell stopped talking and studied her. The silence went

on long enough to make her uncomfortable, yet he didn't seem to mind it at all. She started to feel a little tickle in her head, as if he was looking inside her somehow. But that would be ridiculous.

After several full minutes, she couldn't stand the stillness. "We were running. My husband, my son, and I. They murdered my husband." She hated that tears sprang to her eyes. It was the first clearheaded moment she'd had to look back on what had happened to them. She tried to stuff it deep inside to deal with the emotions later, not in front of this stranger. But he seemed to have already noticed, and yet he still said nothing.

Another two minutes passed, and Teresa felt like she might explode. "I have something they want," she blurted out. "I would not give it to them, and I won't give it to you either!"

Russell nodded, unfazed by her outburst. "It must be supremely important, perhaps for humanity's very survival. You are a scientist."

Teresa felt foolish. These people had saved her life. They were hidden away where the GGP could not find them. The man seemed kind and patient and did not push her. She had to trust *someone*. The treasure she carried was useless if she remained alone.

"I'm… I'm sorry. I don't know who to trust anymore. We've been running a long time."

"Understandable," Russell said. And then the silence again.

"I mean," Teresa continued, "when we realized what they wanted to do, those monsters in the White House, how they were going to just rape the planet and leave it to implode and then move to another celestial world—even bring their own *slaves* with them—we knew we *had* to keep what we discovered secret. It belongs to the *good* people of the Earth, not to those…those…abominations."

Russell's breathing rate increased just a little. "What did you discover?"

Teresa clenched her eyes tightly closed. "All of it," she whispered. "Everything we need to…to leave."

CHAPTER 10

Arnold stepped into the Cabinet Room to find Justine, Brian, and John already seated, along with several other men. It was curious that even with Justine at the helm, they did not seem to employ many women. And everyone was Caucasian, of course. Arnold decided his best strategy for the time being was to say as little as possible until he could see past the facade of what they wanted him to know and figure out the real agenda; he also wanted to get a handle on the pecking order.

Breakfast sat heavy in his gut. That unusual aftertaste, even in his simple eggs and toast, remained with him and was becoming familiar. He realized it was in just about everything he had eaten or drunk here. He wondered if the food was not fresh or if it was hard to get provisions past the pockets of fighting. Resistance combatants did pride themselves on upsetting supply lines and tainting water supplies.

Arnold's head seemed to feel mildly fuzzy all the time now. He guessed he'd get used to it.

No one had bothered to introduce him to the three other men at the table. The conversation was somewhat heated.

"She got away. Her and that half-breed son of hers, but they butchered the husband." The man snickered. "He's the one who knew how to make the enhanced solenoid and its container. Without an adequate power source, she—and whoever she might hope to co-opt—are grounded from the get-go." The speaker was a blond man in his early forties, with a stiff mustache and a southern accent; he seemed amused by the whole situation.

Another stranger spoke up. "Jerry, don't forget, she's a half-breed herself. Just because her skin is lighter don't mean she can pretend to deserve the education she got. Now, if she had cooperated with us, *maybe* we would have even taken that bastard son of hers along. But it doesn't matter. If she wasn't already dead, she couldn't have lived long with a dumdum bullet in her chest, not without medical attention, and where could she have gotten that?"

The blond retorted, "Nice thought, Jansen, but their SUV went over the side of a cliff, a sixty-foot drop. We had a crew comb the area for days. No bodies were found, and no laptops, tablets, or hard drives. No papers. Not so much as a flash drive. Nothing. Where did it all go? Where did *she* go? We've sent a couple of lone scouts out to see if they could pass themselves off as lost resistance fighters needing a safe haven, but so far no one has checked back in with any good news."

Arnold felt Justine's eyes on him, penetrating and purposeful. She placed her elbows on the table, folded her hands in front of her, and said, "Perhaps Mr. Higgins has some knowledge of this."

The room quieted in deference to Justine and all eyes turned to Arnold. He squirmed and started to sweat.

"I… I haven't heard anything." He turned to John for support that was not forthcoming. "We talked about this; I don't know where this 'safe place' for the resistance is supposed to be, except that it's said to be in the mountains somewhere—if it even exists. I had thought it might be out west." He turned back to Justine, trying to hold her gaze but finding it difficult. Gone was the seductress from the other day. This creature in front of him suddenly looked like a wicked sorceress who could squeeze the truth out of anyone with just a thought.

Justine got up from her chair and walked slowly over to Arnold. He noticed her nails then, nearly an inch long and filed to a point on each finger. Her polish was crimson. She was wearing a tight-fitting dress in ice blue that ended above her midthigh. She came alongside the back of his chair on his left side and traced a line on his neck with her index fingernail, stopping just over his carotid, and pressed down slightly.

Arnold felt his breathing increase. He tried to look at her without moving and found it hard to focus on anything. His head was swimming. Maybe he should have skipped breakfast.

Justine lowered her head so that she was speaking directly into his left ear, and the scent of her perfume threatened to choke him. "Maybe we can jog your memory, just a bit. Where did you hear that this place in the mountains was out west? And where did you hear about this place at all?"

"One of my...my functions when I worked at the Pentagon was to blend in with the street people and learn as much as I could and report back. But I never heard anything more than that. It sounded like some made-up fantasy to foster hope in a hopeless situation. Those people are desperate; they need to believe in something." Arnold's speech was rapid, and his voice was shaking. "That was what I came to believe. That it was some stupid, made-up story. No one I talked to had ever actually been there or met anyone who had. I swear it."

Justine pressed harder with her fingernail, and Arnold felt a rush in his head, like the blood flow had been compromised. Then, abruptly, she scratched him hard and walked away. The conversation resumed, but Arnold couldn't follow it. All he could do was breathe.

Distantly, Arnold heard John talking about Enceladus and wondered what Saturn's faraway moon had to do with any of this, but whether it was from Justine's heavy perfume or just general stress, Arnold was too busy fighting to keep himself from passing out to consider the conversation. What the hell was wrong with him?

As the meeting broke up, Arnold reached for his neck, which was sore and itchy. His fingers came away sticky with blood.

CHAPTER 11

Braelyn knocked on Teresa's room. The scientist had been discharged from the hospital wing with her left shoulder in a sling.

"Wanna come for lunch?"

The two women walked up to the huge general dining area in silence. Braelyn and Russell had access to more private dining quarters, of course, but Braelyn wanted to show off some of the vast compound. One wall of the long cafeteria-styled room was made up of triple-layered tempered glass and afforded a heart-stopping view of the valley below and the waterfall to the north. The storm had passed and the sun was blazing, and there was a slight wind causing the top branches to sway. It was late October, and the leaves were a vibrant display of autumn shades, with a scattering of evergreens for accent. It was breathtaking.

"Thank you for coming after us," Teresa said once they

were seated. "I heard it was not a popular choice. But how did you know?"

"Hrmph," Braelyn practically barked. "My brother needs to get his priorities straight. We're not done rescuing people. As for you, I felt you out there."

Braelyn gave her a challenging glare, waiting to see what a scholar like Teresa would do with that information. To Braelyn's surprise, Teresa hardly reacted.

"You have developed your intuitive faculties. That's quite an accomplishment." Teresa raised her eyes to meet Braelyn's for the first time.

Braelyn searched the woman's face. Her intellect was so far beyond anything Braelyn could understand that it was intimidating, and yet she obviously attributed validity to intuition and things "not rational."

"I told my brother we need you. I don't know why, only that we do. Even our little compound is going to be in danger soon."

Teresa took a bite of her pasta. "Neither my son nor I will ever reveal your whereabouts. You needn't worry about that."

"Ha. Actually, sorry to say, you'll never be given a chance to. That's not what I'm talking about. You're a scientist; surely you know this planet is breaking up."

Teresa smiled without looking up from her plate. "So you know."

Braelyn rolled her eyes. "Of course we know. We haven't survived all this time in ignorance. *You* have information we need. I feel it."

Teresa put down her fork and played with her napkin. "I

prefer to say that the planet is reclaiming itself. The Earth will go on, just in a different form. And…without us."

"That's what Russell says."

"I have a lot of trepidation about sharing what we discovered. And yet," she said, gazing off out the window at the waterfall, looking for a moment as if she were mostly talking to herself, "if I don't share it somewhere, it's all a waste." She looked back at Braelyn. "My research partner and my husband were both murdered for this information. The GGP want it desperately. I… I don't want their lives to have been lost in vain."

"Can you be sure they didn't find it?"

Teresa smiled and shook her head, as if she was remembering a sick joke.

"There was nothing left to find. We wiped the computers and burned the entire lab. I brought the only physical specimen we created with us into the mountains, and what Devon transferred onto the flash drive is missing some key components that now exist," she tapped her temple with her right index finger, "only in my head. The papers you found in our pack were there in case I did not make it. On the surface, the plans look like a sturdy ship, so if they were confiscated, it would appear to be the real thing, but without the information on the flash drive, it will not survive the stresses of accelerating into a warp bubble."

"Warp bub—" Braelyn's jaw slackened in spite of herself. "Is it possible?" she whispered.

Teresa looked as if she feared she had said too much. She returned to her pasta and focused on eating her meal with only one hand, and in truth, Braelyn knew Teresa needed to restore her strength from her ordeal, so she remained quiet and let her finish her lunch, but she had dozens of questions! Russell needed to be here.

As if on cue, Russell walked over carrying a tray of vegetarian stew and the compound's tasty whole grain bread. "May I join you?"

Russell told them that Devon was in the gym with Amira, who was training him in personal defense tactics. Amira was the best; he was in good hands.

Teresa frowned. "Yes, but had he known those things, he might have tried to fight back against the Marauders, and no matter how good his training, he was no match for guns and shovels."

"You might be surprised," Russell said. Then he put the plans for the ship on the table.

"I hope you don't mind that I examined these. We are desperate for information."

It was Teresa's turn to be silent and wait for Russell to speak.

"This is a lovely ship," Russell said. "But it will never make it to the far reaches of outer space. It wouldn't even make it to the moon."

Now Teresa's jaw dropped, and Braelyn smirked. Her brother's mental ability never shocked her, but he sure had that effect on others.

"Tell me about it. Please," he said.

Teresa visibly made up her mind, and she started to explain. Once she did, it was as if she couldn't stop.

She revealed that the GGP's inner circle was investigating escape routes to get off the planet. She and her research partner had been working on Miguel Alcubierre's equations created in the 1990s. He was able to establish the conditions necessary to develop a warp bubble, which would expand the universe behind an object while contracting it in front, essentially twisting space and propelling the object forward at the speed of light or faster. It was based on the theory of relativity and assumed a ship would act the same as a particle in those equations. But of course, a ship has vastly greater mass.

Braelyn noticed her brother in intense concentration as Teresa went on, soaking up the information that might be coming faster than even he could handle. When he spoke up, Braelyn was surprised that he seemed to be keeping up so well.

"But nothing travels faster than the speed of light. Nothing we know of, anyway," Russell commented.

"Not true. Neutrinos travel faster than the speed of light. *Thought* travels faster than the speed of light. As do tachyons. These things, though never actually measured—for obvious reasons—are all believed to travel as fast or faster.

"You realize, Russell, that Time as we know it, stops at light speed." Teresa let that sink in for a minute.

"Yes, but at the speed of light, mass goes to zero, right? How can an object with no mass have any momentum to propel it forward?" Russell asked.

"Right you are. The particle ceases to be a particle and becomes pure energy. And that energy can propagate, *as a wave*. Like photons versus light waves, the forms are interchangeable, each obeying their own laws, but they are both aspects of the same substance. Are you sure you've had no training in physics?"

In typical snarky style, Braelyn chimed in. "So why hasn't everyone gone off on a *Star Trek* voyage yet?"

Teresa turned to Braelyn and gave her a calm, knowing smile. "The energy requirements are insurmountable for this model, at this time."

Her words hung in the air.

"Okay, I'll bite," Braelyn finally said. "Sounds like you've solved that. You found another model."

Teresa got very serious. "Not me. Erik Lentz. He reworked the equations, postulating instead of just the twisting, contracting, and expanding model of space in the warp bubble, the creation of a soliton wave for propagation."

Russell turned to a perplexed Braelyn. "Solitons are waves that travel like ripples in water. The water stays relatively still but the wave front moves; the *energy* moves. A tsunami is a soliton with a very large wavelength. The water rises and falls, but it does not move horizontally across the ocean. It is self-reinforcing and maintains its shape and constant velocity with little to no energy expenditure once it's been generated. Until, that is, it runs out of water and crashes into the continent."

Russell turned to Teresa. "This can work? We can generate the energy for this?"

"My colleague and I thought so but not for the more traditional warp bubble. For that, we would need negative energy, maybe antimatter, and the storage of such energy is also a problem. But for a soliton, we were looking into gamma radiation. We need to store a lot of it; the challenge is that it has such a short wavelength, it tends to cut through most any substance very quickly. Although, if we can contain enough of it, it could supply the energy we need *and* we could use it to charge photovoltaic cells; plus it would be readily available from any star system we pass. We've constructed a storage chamber of sorts…"

Braelyn tuned them out. She just couldn't keep up with this level of discussion. There was a time when she would have scolded herself for being too stupid to follow scientific discourse, but she had grown a lot over the last decade, and she recognized there were few people who could catch more than an inkling of what Teresa was talking about. She did compliment herself on knowing how much they needed Teresa. Her presence in the compound was entirely due to Braelyn's insistence. When she got up to leave, Russell and Teresa were so engrossed in their focused dialogue, they didn't even notice she was gone.

Braelyn wandered down to the holding area where Sahina Keter was being housed. She knocked and entered.

Sahina was sitting calmly on the bed, feet up and back propped against the headboard, reading *Stranger in a Strange Land* by Robert Heinlein. Braelyn was again struck by the androgenous nature of this person, and she was doubly impressed to find her visitor reading; she didn't think books were generally available these days. Sahina barely looked up when she came in.

Braelyn cleared her throat and sat down on a chair. "How are you finding your stay here?"

Sahina slipped a bookmark between the pages and put the novel aside. "I am very appreciative of being brought in out of the rain, but I hadn't realized I would be kept prisoner, I must admit." When Braelyn did not answer, he added, "I *am* a prisoner, yes?"

His voice sounded deep and masculine, and well-defined muscles flexed as he put the book down. Yes, definitely male.

"We can't risk anyone finding out where we are. So I guess that's true. We can't let you leave."

"Why can't you just 'wipe my mind' and send me away? Rumor has it you have this capacity."

"Huh?"

"I said," Sahina repeated patiently, "rumor has it that you, or some among you, have the capacity to enter people's minds, determine whether they are telling the truth, if they are under the influence of any chemical factors, and also to wipe their minds clean. If you wish to."

Braelyn squinted at him. Her thoughts were racing. Almost no one outside the compound knew that Russell's and her perceptual functions were accelerated by the drug they were exposed to as small children. And only the few with a need to know inside the compound had any idea. Unless they had been involved in that discovery from the beginning, like the psychiatrist, Dr. Mitchell Gray. Amira had admirably pieced it together herself, but Braelyn doubted she spoke of it here. And if she was somehow in touch with her previous home base in Israel, it was not known—at least not to Braelyn. Anyway, Sahina did not appear to be Israeli—his accent was all wrong, and he didn't *feel* the part. He wasn't from any Western country either, for that matter. Braelyn couldn't place him at all, and that irked her. In any event, "wiping minds" was hogwash, and she said so.

Braelyn sunk into herself for a moment and reached out mentally to Sahina. She had tried this at their first encounter and had found only a person who was fatigued and cold from the elements. This time she pushed further and met with something odd. She couldn't identify it. He was not dishonest, but there was something…opaque. Like he was hiding some part of himself, or as if his mind was on a different plane to which Braelyn had no access. No one had been able to hide from her like this before.

He looked at her with a bland expression. Did he know she had just tried to sense him? Braelyn often wondered if people could feel her probing.

"How did you happen to be in the mountains, alone, with no supplies when we found you? We're a bit off the beaten path," Braelyn said.

"I was hiking and got lost."

"That's bullshit. Do you think we're stupid? You look like a spy. And you appeared, like, out of thin air. Who else knows you were out 'hiking'? I only let you in because you could have given us away. But you had to have intended to report back to someone about your findings."

Sahina sat calmly with his hands folded in his lap. Or *her* lap. As Braelyn watched, *she* started to look more and more feminine. The muscles in her arms were well defined, yes, but the musculature suddenly looked overall smaller. The face more delicate. Braelyn didn't give a rat's behind if this guy was male, female, or android, LGBT or undecided. But she couldn't seem to focus enough to get a solid picture of who this Sahina Keter was. It was exasperating her. Like trying to see clearly through a mist. The more she strained to see, the more fluid the image became. The shoulder-length brown hair, which had been smooth as silk when Braelyn had walked in, now seemed infused with humidity, and as Sahina's hands ran through it, it looked bushier.

Sahina was obviously not going to say anything further

about her "hike," even though the answer did not make much sense. Russell was going to have to resort to his own examination technique and check this guy—or girl—out. Braelyn was regretting the impulsive decision to bring her into the compound. But what else could they have done? They'd nearly lost Teresa as it was.

CHAPTER 12

evon felt he was making great strides learning self-defense techniques. He was fit, even if his musculature was slight, had always been a great pupil, and he was so hungry for this knowledge. Amira showed him how he could use his slender build to his advantage, by being quick and using the opponent's energy and momentum to his own benefit. If only he had known this stuff before! Maybe he could have saved Dad. He let his thoughts stray and caught Amira's glove on his chin.

"You must never let your concentration lapse," she said. "The enemy will look for the slightest hesitation and take advantage. You have good reflexes when you stay focused."

"I'm sorry. I was just thinking—"

"I know what you were thinking. But it does not serve you now. Regrets and tears will get you killed, and that is a poor tribute to those you have lost. You must be strong now.

Ready at a moment's notice. Never let your guard down, not even in sleep."

Devon straightened up. "Do you never rest?"

"Rest, yes. Relax, as you know it, no. I rest in heightened meditation that leaves a part of me on the lookout."

"Even here, where it's safe? That sounds almost inhuman. And exhausting. With no hope for peace."

Amira softened. "I have watched too many die. I will relax when the enemy has been destroyed." She shrugged. "I'm sorry, you don't have to be as tough as I am. But you are at the beginning of a long and arduous journey; you should be prepared. I want you to survive." Amira took off her boxing gloves. "Come, let's get some lunch."

Devon looked around curiously as Amira led him, not to the main dining area, but to a smaller café of sorts. They collected their meals and sat at a table in the rear. Devon noticed that Amira placed her back to the corner and quickly and unobtrusively surveilled the room before turning to her food. She had been teaching him to do the same, but this was the first that he noticed how second nature it was for her; she didn't even seem to realize she was doing it.

"You've been running for a long time," Devon said.

Amira looked at him and their eyes locked. Devon felt a sudden connection to her, and he sensed tremendous pain in her past. He didn't know what to say, but he couldn't seem to look away either. She seemed like she was going to speak—to explain—but at the last second, she just shook her head slightly and broke the contact.

The silence became awkward.

"You're not from here. From Israel, they told me? Are you in touch with your family from back home? How did you manage to stay when they closed the borders? I thought they had deported everyone."

"You ask a lot of questions, you know that?"

Devon lowered his head and focused on his vegetarian burger. He'd noticed there wasn't a lot of meat served in the complex, and he supposed it would be hard to farm animals for food in such a small, restricted area, but he did miss his old food choices.

Amira watched him with his lunch and chuckled. "Get used to it. There's no room for ranches or chicken farms here, and when we go off-world, we will not be taking animals for slaughter. Only grain, seeds, and the hope that they will germinate in alien soil if we find nothing suitable there to eat."

Devon had no idea if he could trust this woman, but Amira *had* saved his life, and here she was teaching him to defend himself. Of all the people he had met recently, she seemed the least interested in getting something from him in return. And he felt her isolation and her loneliness. She was also a stranger here, right?

"My parents were working on the logistics of such a plan..." he ventured hesitantly.

"I am not proficient in the strategy of that journey, should it come to pass. I am trained to be a survivor, wherever you plunk me down. That is my skill."

"Survival here will soon not be an option," Devon said. "My father compared this country to Sodom and Gomorrah, filled with iniquity. He said it would ultimately be destroyed, that it was God's will that we leave it behind and not look back. Ever."

"Afraid you will be turned into a pillar of salt, like Lot's wife?"

"My father believed that those who have turned their backs on God's law to stare with longing at this depravity are already as cold and empty as pillars of salt. Inhuman. Soulless. No better than grains of sand," Devon said. "He was not afraid to die. I just wish…"

Amira reached across the table and touched Devon's hand but then turned quickly back to her lunch. The silence stretched.

"How did you end up with these people?" Devon asked.

Amira frowned. "I guess it's not really a secret, but Russell hates to talk about it. His wife, Maya, was so incredibly sensitive to manipulation and control by the GGP with their use of scopolamine to compel a person to do their bidding. It wasn't her fault, you understand, just her particular neurochemistry. They got to her on one of her trips into town to purchase supplies, back in the mid 2020s. Gave her a huge dose and interrogated her, and then directed her to come back and sabotage the food supplies. I was eavesdropping and when I observed her heading back without the provisions she was supposed to purchase, I followed her. She…she didn't smell right. How can I say it in English? I told you, I'm a survivor. Survivors use *all* our senses."

She stopped talking and drank from her water bottle. She kept shaking her head as she remembered what happened next.

"She was definitely up to no good. I didn't know who she was then, but my undercover assignment had been to track the contact who dosed her. When I heard the command Maya was given, I let the source go and followed her. When she got here… I knew it was a disaster in the making. She turned around… I'll never forget her eyes. She just wasn't present. Something inhuman was looking back at me. She pulled a knife…"

Devon was shocked. Not just by the story as it unfolded, but because he sensed that her naked display of emotion was an extreme rarity.

Amira looked up at him, and for a split second, she was just a scared, vulnerable child. "I told you. I'm a survivor. She came at me with the knife. And she would not allow me to just subdue her. She struggled so fiercely; I hardly knew where she got the strength.

"I killed her. It was not my intention, but it was her or me. And the strangest thing, Russell came bounding out of the mountainside—I didn't even know there was a gate there— still wouldn't be able to find it without knowing exactly what to look for. He came with armed men. Like he felt her distress somehow…and her death.

"I thought he would kill me for it, but he just looked at me. He looked *into* me. And he knew somehow. He asked me what happened and I told him, but he wasn't the least surprised. I had no idea she was his *wife*. But he just took me inside and I've been here since. That was at least four years ago. And since that day, virtually no one leaves the compound. Not for any reason. If you come here, you stay here."

They sat in silence for a while. Devon didn't know what to say. "So you weren't here on 'vacation'? That's what I heard."

"No, not at all. But only Russell knows that. I owed that to him, and he has kept it quiet—not that I think it matters now. They did shut down all transportation so that return to *ha'aretz*, to Israel, was not an option without raising significant international attention and involving my government—and maybe not even then. I might have been taken prisoner instead. In this compound, only Russell knows." She smiled at Devon. "And now you. It is like I owe him a debt. I took his wife, so I give him my service. My people know and approve. And perhaps one day I will meet them again on another world."

"And you are telling…me?"

Amira shrugged and looked into his eyes. "I feel I can trust you," she said and smiled.

Devon thought her smile was the most beautiful thing he had ever seen.

CHAPTER 13

Arnold's head was swimming when he got back to his office. When he applied for this position, it was with sincere interest in joining and helping the GGP. He hadn't ever thought about who they really were or what they were about. He wanted to work in government, and this was the current government.

At thirty years old, Arnold thought he was making a nice career for himself. Since he could remember, he had wanted to contribute to the presiding administration in a meaningful way. He had dual majored in political science and engineering, and upon graduation, he was fortunate enough to get a job as an intern at the Pentagon. That was in 2024, just as the balance of power was shifting back to the conservatives in the United States. Ironically, Arnold hadn't bothered himself much with political affiliations; he just wanted to work near the greatest seat of power in the world.

His parents were humble people. His father, and his father

before him, were coal miners, and that's all they knew. Under the liberals, coal was being devalued in favor of cleaner forms of energy, and Arnold's father blamed the government for stealing his livelihood. When it became clear that Arnold had a great aptitude for math, he went off to college—the first in his family to do so—and he was determined to make his father proud, even though that always seemed to feel like a losing battle.

College life had created some confusion. The trouble-maker kids would protest so many things. Gay rights, rights to an abortion, rights of Blacks… Arnold just didn't care about any of that. He was a smart, privileged White boy who had been given a scholarship for his brains, and he didn't want to jeopardize that by getting involved in issues that had nothing to do with him. And he didn't care a wit who commanded the current regime, as long as he could work there.

He married Hannah at twenty-six, and they had little Eve right away. So any job that put food on the table was good by Arnold. They never talked politics, so he hadn't even known if she had an opinion about the GGP until her sister caught a virus just after getting pregnant with a much-wanted child.

It was within a month of Arnold and Hannah getting married. Jaelle and her husband had been trying for years, and they were all overjoyed when Jaelle found out. But within a few weeks, the virus had attacked her heart, and Jaelle's obstetrician told her that she was in grave danger. As the baby grew, it made greater and greater demands on her cardiac output, and Jaelle became short of breath, dizzy, and tired all the time. By the time she was thirteen weeks, it was obvious even to Hannah that her sister was going to die from this pregnancy.

The obstetrician said she wanted to perform an abortion but was afraid. Under the current rule, there were no circumstances for which an abortion was legal, and worse than losing her medical license, the obstetrician could be put to death. She did refer Jaelle to an underground network that would do such things, but Jaelle put it off. She was already so sick, and she had been told that if she developed an infection from the procedure, in her present state, she could become septic and die.

By the time Hannah's sister was fifteen weeks, both she and her baby were dead.

Hannah cried and protested the governmental laws, but Arnold shrugged it off and said it was the law of the land. Besides, it must be God's will. The relationship between Arnold and Hannah changed after that, and they argued frequently. Arnold began to fear that if she became too vocal about her anger regarding her sister, she could put them all in danger, but after a while, Hannah just stopped talking about it. Until her comment: "That depends on who's writing the history."

Four months ago, Arnold was approached by a couple of men saying they could influence his application status for chief of staff and get him in. They said he would be expected to play a certain role and did not elaborate on what that role would be but assured him it was all in keeping with the greater good of society. First, he had to be accepted by Justine Ganaffe—that was step one. More would be revealed once he was inside. Arnold was just not a suspicious person; he would have done most anything if he was promised success, and true to their word, he soon received an invitation to interview. The men returned shortly after and prepped him on what would likely be expected of him and how best to succeed.

Despite her sister's ill fortune, Hannah had always been supportive of him, up until little Eve was born. Then her motherly instincts took over, and she started asking a lot of uncomfortable questions that Arnold felt were best left alone. It was abundantly obvious that the only way to survive these days was to tow the party line. If she started voicing concerns out loud, there was no telling what might happen to her and the baby.

And then his life turned upside down.

Those days, he worked undercover in DC and Baltimore. He patrolled the streets, listening for rumors and signs of dissent, and he saw such filth in the people living in the gutter. They all seemed stupid to him. Why were they fighting the Great Ganaffe? There were so many jobs now that manufacturing and coal mining were back in production. Even his father returned to work, old as he was.

Arnold flashed back to the moment it had all changed for him, only a few weeks before his application had been chosen for this position. He was staked out on a trash-littered street one night, when he heard little meows coming from behind a dumpster. Some stupid cat, he thought, and he wanted to go shut it up before it gave away his position. As he considered doing so, muted footsteps came running around the corner and headed toward the dumpster. The cat became quiet, and emerging from the back of the garbage bin, appeared a little Black girl, maybe seven or eight, wearing dirty, tattered clothes and holding a kitten. Her mother came running up, scolded her in whispers to leave the cat and come away quick, but the little girl would not go without the kitten.

The next minute, Whispies rode up on motorcycles and surrounded the woman, the child, and the cat. The mother fell to her knees, pleading, saying her daughter meant no harm, just a little girl, but the Whispies shoved the mother aside and lifted the child by her shirt collar. She dropped the cat, who ran off, as the Whispies took turns raping the little girl and making the mother watch, before shooting them each in the belly.

After they left, Arnold walked over to the little girl. She was barely alive and was trying to whisper something. He leaned over to her, and she said, "Please help Tiger. He was just hungry, he didn't know. He's just a baby…"

Then she closed her eyes, and she was gone.

That night changed everything for Arnold. That night he began to care. That little girl who seemed to have no thought for herself or even her mother, but to whom a tiny, vulnerable creature was worth dying for, stayed with him. Her image swam in front of his face like an accusation every night when he was trying to sleep. Why should this affect him so when his sister-in-law's death did not? Arnold still didn't understand what it meant, but he knew he was different after that. And to what avail? He had put in his application months earlier. To turn it down now would mean drawing a spotlight of suspicion over himself. He'd probably be killed.

Was that why he didn't seem to fit in here now? How could some trivial encounter with a little Black girl and her kitten change him in any meaningful way? He tried to concentrate on obliterating the vision from his mind. He didn't even like cats! Spiteful, uncooperative animals who'd scratch your eyes out if you weren't good to them.

But the more he tried to reconstitute his feelings of hate toward the Black community and the small, annoying creatures of the Earth, the harder it was. He tried chanting the mantra: "Great Ganaffe for a Great America," but it was more elusive than ever. He began to panic then, wondering how he would keep this new personal flaw from the probing eyes of the GGP, and now, from Justine Ganaffe and his new comrades in arms as well. He knew if they suspected he had even the slightest divergence of thought from the party, he would be executed in a heartbeat.

But he hadn't deviated from the party! He was still a most loyal servant, and he was on track to do his life's calling. Kittens and small children were irrelevant!

There was a knock on the door, and before Arnold could answer, an angry John Sentics walked in.

"What the hell was that? Why do you look like you're holding back on us? You really need to tell Justine *everything* you know. And don't wait for her to ask; volunteer it. You looked guilty as sin in there. You won't be around for a week if you keep up that shit."

"But I *don't* know anything. I told you that! I wasn't lying. Why would I hold back? We can't let a place like that stay operational, I get it. I don't know what's wrong with me… my head feels fuzzy all the time, and my stomach… It's like I ate some bad food or something. Maybe I'm allergic to something they cook with here."

John suddenly burst out laughing, which confused Arnold even more. "Are you an 'ultrasensitive' then? Some people have too strong a reaction to the scops in the food."

He looked at Arnold's completely perplexed expression. "You didn't know about the scops? You've been eating it all your life, unless you grow your own food, and who would do that?"

John suddenly peered at him intensely. "Unless…are you one of the organic folk? But that would mean—those people are all in the resistance. Are you a traitor then?"

"No! Of course not. I'm one hundred percent supportive of the GGP. That's why I applied for this job. I even left my family to chase my childhood dream, and it led me here. What's a 'scop' anyway?"

"Scopolamine," John said. "It's the drug in all the food. Completely necessary, it keeps the people in line. Well, maybe the scops are stronger this side of the White House walls. I guess we could start bringing you upstairs to eat with us. It's a little early, and you haven't been completely vetted yet, but you're already headed for elimination if you don't straighten up fast. Maybe if we let your head clear, your memory will get jogged."

Arnold felt the pit in his stomach expand. How could his career end like this? After less than a week.

"What can I do? I want to make this work."

John shrugged. "I'd suggest you go seek out Justine and apologize to her. Tell her you weren't feeling well. Then give her some information she will be happy to have. I'm sure you have some useful knowledge to share. If you don't… well, she won't be needing you around anyway."

John's words were cryptic and icy. He turned on his heel and walked out of the room.

CHAPTER 14

Russell had spent the entire afternoon with Teresa, and for the first time that he could remember, his head was spinning from information overload. Not like when he was a child, and he would need extra time to put things in their appropriate place in his mind, but from the impact of the possibilities the information invited. Question upon question grew so that he was overwhelmed with excitement, doubt, hope, and trepidation, all at the same time.

He learned that the GGP was looking at Saturn's moon, Enceladus, as a place to settle. That moon was a relatively recent discovery, but it appeared to hold promise for supporting human life. It was a bit on the cold side and believed to harbor ice volcanoes, but the likelihood of water on the surface made it the most favorable alternate celestial body in their solar system. It was estimated to be 790.1 million miles away, and travel would take between thirty-eight and sixty-eight months, depending on where Earth and Saturn were in their orbits when the journey began.

Teresa said she wasn't sure President Martine Ganaffe would make it on that journey, but she wasn't even sure the man was still alive. GGP crews had already been sent to scout the moon and start building. Those crews, according to Teresa, were slated to become slaves once the settlement was operational, which the workers largely suspected, but they had agreed to go because it afforded them the prospect of survival. The Earth would soon be uninhabitable by mammalian species of any kind, and the "volunteers" were heavily drugged from early on, before they even began to prepare for the trip.

Teresa and her team had been directed to look at faster-than-light travel to Enceladus, along with neighboring star systems for the obvious reasons, but her team had secretly been exploring other options, assuming warp speed could be accomplished. Enceladus was a moon, not a planet, and it was not near the Goldilocks Zone, which would be immensely more desirable, that sweet spot in a solar system that was at optimal distance from its star to afford the most agreeable temperatures to Earth mammals and the plants that sustained them.

If light speed could be accomplished by the GGP (and if Teresa and her colleagues could achieve it, they couldn't rule out the Ganaffe Party following suit), they would undoubtedly look at the neighboring solar system of Alpha Centauri. In secret, Teresa and her partners explored beyond to other solar systems; getting as far away from the GGP as possible seemed more appealing.

While Alpha Centauri was the closest system, the Cygnus

constellation indicated the existence of Kepler 186, the next closest star that showed promise of Earth-size planets. Its sun had less metal content and appeared to be a red dwarf, cooler than Earth's Sol, but of the planets that were thought to exist there, it looked like a good chance one of them would support human life. And there was another system in the Cygnus vicinity and one in the Lyra constellation that were of interest as well.

If they could make this vessel carry them at warp speed, and *if* they could muster and store the energy required to do so, and *if* they could get the ship out into orbit without being shot down—because it was not possible to initiate light speed from ground level without wreaking havoc behind them on the planet's surface—how would they choose their destination? There *were* several choices, but all of them were maybes; nothing was guaranteed to support human life.

There were just too many "ifs" for comfort.

Any new planet had to be evaluated for water content, air composition, gravity, and temperature. Just for starts. And then, if it would support them, wouldn't there be a high likelihood that there was already sapient life on its surface? How would that go over, if they showed up to carve out space on a planet that was already inhabited by another species? How would people of the Earth have responded to a shipload of aliens setting down in, say, Oklahoma? Russell shuddered at that thought.

Russell needed help. And every option he looked at sent him to the same place: The shaman from his past. Even though the theory that he had been given assistance through some divine intervention twelve years ago did not jibe with his purely rational perspective, he knew *something* had contrived to pluck him and his little community out of the clutches of the GGP. *El Curandero Grande.* It all led back to him.

How could Russell even find him? Was he still alive? The psychiatrist, Dr. Mitchell Gray, had researched the tribes in the Northern Peruvian Andes, particularly in Peoria where Russell's family had vacationed so long ago, and he found that their shaman was thought by some to be two hundred years old. Some rumors had it that he was not even human. Just rumors, of course. And yet, this…this figure had foretold that Russell would become another *curandero grande*, like himself.

Russell rummaged doggedly through his memories of his journey of self-discovery and attempt at understanding the forces that had been at work in his life at that time. He had not thought seriously about it in years. He had not felt the presence of the shaman, nor heard from the mysterious man named Harris, also known as Horatius Marsden, since they moved into the Catskills compound twelve years ago. But something must be keeping them safe. Keeping them hidden. It was unreasonable to think that after all these years, the GGP would not have found them, that the enormous weapons supply they were given never needed to be used. What were the chances that was all coincidental?

He sat back down with the notes he had taken when he spoke to Teresa. Alpha Centauri, Proxima Centauri, Cygnus… His head swam, and he quailed with the burden of responsibility he felt for the couple of thousand people living with them. Was it really all up to him? How could he lead these people by himself?

CHAPTER 15

Joshua Plessman, Braelyn's son, had also grown immensely since the "before-time," as Joshua thought of it. Twelve years ago, unknown to his aunt and uncle, he was intentionally given scopolamine as part of a learning program, but he had later become a victim of the dust from the pure Devil's Breath flower, having been in the wrong place at the wrong time.

His lack of scholarly aptitude, or as the less politically correct would say, his low-functioning intellect, had improved impressively through the program. And then after he was deliberately drugged to make him forget a murder he had witnessed, and after his uncle Russell—who was just discovering his own psychic abilities—had instinctively removed the effects of the drug, Joshua had even further developed a mental acuity that surprised and sometimes scared him. Yet he had never lost the emotional innocence that he had shrouded himself in, probably to avoid directly facing the trials of his childhood. For all that, he still did not see himself as being smart.

As a child, Joshua had been left largely to fend for himself while his mother led a life of drugs and depravity until he was formally taken in by his aunt and uncle at the age of ten. Later, he realized his behavior in his first quarter of a century of life was mostly a desperate attempt to draw his mother back to him by making himself small and sweet in an unconscious attempt to avoid being a burden.

Now, at thirty-six years old, Joshua was still no genius. But he did have a solid comprehension of how to manage the farming network they had on the valley floor, something he could not have mastered in his early twenties. He had basic knowledge of solar panels, the windmill generator, and the variety of machinery they used to harvest the crops. He organized tasks for members of the Sustenance Team, as they were called, and kept track of where they were in their daily supplies. They were the ones who fed everyone in the compound, and as such, were given high status in the community, even though it did not take a college degree to do this work.

He was on the ground as wheat was being gathered and scanning the skies for spy planes or helicopters. It was one of his favorite jobs, mostly because he loved looking up at the open air. He missed the feeling of being free to wander, and he made up adventures in his head while he gazed.

Joshua understood that it was important to keep an eye out, but he was puzzled because nothing ever seemed to fly over them—except birds, of course. When he had once asked his uncle why that was, Russell had just grinned and said they were extraordinarily lucky. It was one of those moments when Joshua was sure he had missed the meaning of something but was too shy to question it further.

As Joshua surveilled the grounds next, he noticed an unfamiliar figure drifting around between the rows of corn. In his disarmingly friendly way, Joshua ambled over to greet him.

"Hey, buddy. What'ya up to? I've never seen you out here before. You interested in joining the Sustenance Team?"

"Just looking around," the man said.

"What's your name? I'm Joshua."

The man turned to Joshua, and suddenly Joshua was afraid—he couldn't say of what. To be honest, he hadn't been afraid of much of anything since they had settled down in this little oasis in the mountains. The feeling instantly brought back memories of the before-time. Before he had gotten smart. Before his friend Donny had been killed. Before he had been sort of reborn into a brain that could puzzle things out but that felt a little like he was wearing the wrong size.

"My name is Sahina. Sahina Keter."

"Oh," Joshua said. He couldn't seem to figure what else to say, not generally one of his problems. Usually, people said he talked too much.

Sahina just nodded at him knowingly for a minute and then smiled and turned back to his meanderings.

"Wait." Joshua ran to catch up with him. "Are you...are you supposed to be here?"

"Of course," Sahina said, and he smiled.

Joshua was confused. They never saw new people out here. It was pretty much a closed society. His mom had told him she had rescued a couple of scientists recently, a mother and son pair. Joshua was hoping maybe the son would be a new friend, if he didn't mind Joshua being less clever than he was, but he hadn't heard about anyone else who was new.

He was suddenly distracted by Ricardo, who was making his daily pass in the valley. Ricardo was in charge of structural security, which meant keeping an eye on weather changes, the Richter scale, and atmospheric toxins, like those from forest fires and volcanoes—although, thankfully, there weren't many volcanoes local to them—but ash from fire was frequently a threat. Everything growing in the valley had to be rinsed down after those showers. Joshua had learned how interconnected they all were, even in their little enclave, when he realized that the skies did not recognize man-made boundaries.

Joshua loved Ricardo. He saw him nearly every day, and Ricardo always made sure Joshua understood everything he was doing, and he would make a game of it. Not just how to do tasks, but why. They saw each other more now than Joshua saw either his mother or his uncle. Joshua thought Ricardo was a great father to his two kids, who were seven and nine. Joshua had lost his own father before he was even born, and even though his uncle Russell was always there, and Joshua never wanted to complain, he secretly longed for someone to call Dad. Ricardo was nearly the same age as Joshua, but in Joshua's mind, the other man was much older and more mature.

He ran off after Ricardo and completely forgot about the stranger named Sahina.

CHAPTER 16

Arnold's mouth was dry as he looked around his little office. He'd been informed that he was chosen for a prestigious mission, and he should prepare. He might not be coming back to the White House for a long time, which made him suspicious. Hadn't he been told he was never going to leave this building again? What exactly *did* happen to people who didn't "work out"?

He had asked if it might be possible to see his family and got only a smirk in return. He sighed. He pulled out a small backpack and began to throw in a couple of fresh shirts, socks, and underwear, and shortly, there was a knock on the door.

A man walked in and sized Arnold up quickly. He didn't introduce himself, just offered a cursory query.

"Arnold Higgins?"

"Yes, that's me." Arnold thought his voice sounded like a frog croaking.

"This is what's going to happen: We are going to go downstairs and get you suited up in more appropriate attire. You need to blend in with the resistance. Then we'll give you a water bottle and a granola bar and drop you off in the mountains in the vicinity of where we last received a transmission. Just before you embark, we will have you smoke a pipe. The substance in the pipe will make you impervious to any attempt to hijack your thoughts to use against us. In short, you may not remember much after that."

Arnold didn't know what to say. Would there be poison in the pipe? It seemed an inefficient way to kill him. If they wanted him gone, they needn't go to such trouble to make him feel like he was going to be aiding the GGP. They could just take him out back and shoot him.

"What will I be doing, sir?"

"We will explain that to you once you embark. And Higgins. You will be doing a great service. Make no mistake."

They headed down the hall, and the zombie guard who always watched his room fell into step behind them. Odd, since he had seemed permanently stationed outside Arnold's room. So much so that Arnold had nearly ceased to register his presence. As they continued to the elevator, two more blank-faced guards joined them. By the time they got to the ground floor, Arnold's heart was racing, and he was sweating. He was led into a small room in an alcove off the main hall, and the unidentified man who had fetched him handed him a T-shirt, an overshirt, a pair of blue jeans, and a dark brown hoodie.

Arnold changed and found the clothes comfortably warm. He was handed a waterproof jacket and given the water bottle and granola bar to put in his pockets. At a glance, it looked like the water bottle was no longer sealed. But maybe that went along with his persona; someone who couldn't afford water but had to refill an empty found lying on the street somewhere.

Next, they handed him the pipe.

Arnold held it at arm's length and took a deep breath. He was nothing short of terrified. He tried to meet the eyes of the man who had brought him this far, but he wouldn't return Arnold's gaze. Arnold wondered why he wasn't even told the man's name, and started to ask, but he was interrupted.

"Go ahead, smoke it. It doesn't hurt."

So Arnold smoked.

The room seemed to shift and become…dull. Like he was seeing everything through dirty cellophane. Arnold had smoked pot in his youth, but this was nothing like that. Everything remained as it was, except that he had a tremendous urge to take off his glasses and clean them—and he wasn't even wearing glasses.

Vaguely, he became aware that the man was talking to him, without any concern about whether Arnold was even listening. He wanted to stop him, ask him to repeat—how was he supposed to know what to do when he missed his first few sentences? But now the man was just giving him a half-smile and a reassuring nod.

The next thing Arnold knew, he was boarding a helicopter with his three blank-faced escorts and flying over rich foliage, some green and some turning orange, yellow, and red. Wasn't the fall beautiful? The helicopter hovered a foot from the ground over a small clear patch, and they all jumped down to the forest floor. Then the copter rose in the air and was gone.

Arnold had no idea where he was. His companions

seemed tuned into his every move, but they did not speak. He searched through his backpack, which had been reorganized. Gone were his previous clean clothes, and in their place was a high frequency radio, a camera, a small blanket, a compass, and a bare-bones map. He now remembered he was to seek out this Safe Place and infiltrate it unnoticed.

Since he had no idea where he was, and no one seemed to know where this resistance hold was, it was pretty hard to choose a direction to start. He began walking downhill, mostly because it was an easier hike, but one of the guards moved swiftly to block his path. His alacrity surprised Arnold. He had assumed these quasi humans were as slow physically as they were mentally. He tried talking to them again.

"Do you know which direction I'm supposed to go?"

No answer. Arnold tried to step around him, but the creature moved again to block him.

"Well, I guess not that way. It would sure be easier if you guys would speak to me, since you seem to know where to go," Arnold said aloud but mostly to himself, hardly expecting an answer.

"Go up," the guard spoke. Its voice sounded quite normal, which was startling in itself. Arnold was expecting something machinelike to match its behavior.

"Okay," Arnold said and nodded. As he turned uphill, all three guards fell into step with him, on each side and behind him. He now saw their firearms, nifty little semiautomatics that had been under their jackets, which they now held at the ready. Why didn't he get one of those?

As they continued slowly but inexorably uphill, the temperature dropped, and a mist began to fall. Arnold put on the waterproof jacket and lifted the hoodie over his head. Suddenly, the three zombies stopped as one and raised their weapons.

Arnold hadn't seen anything, and he was trying to process how these three acted in complete synchronicity, as if they were of one mind. It made him think of the Borg from a long-ago *Star Trek* episode—before viewing that stuff became prohibited by the GGP. It seemed like a lifetime ago.

Arnold peered through the now foggy forest as carefully as he could, but he couldn't see anything. It wasn't until the zombies turned their backs to Arnold to face outward, forming a circle, that he saw the ring of animals in the perimeter, just out of sight. There were snarls coming from several sides at once. Arnold froze. And then the coyotes pounced.

There must have been at least seven or eight, and they were as organized as the blank-faced sentries, looking to catch the little troop off guard. Bullets were fired in a rush, and the coyotes feinted and turned. Two of them caught one of the mindless men from the side. He was knocked over by one while the other sunk its teeth into his throat. He died so quickly, Arnold barely had time to register it. Now those same coyotes were coming for Arnold, and he had nothing to defend himself with. Instinctively, he threw his left arm up in front of his face, expecting to feel the sharp teeth of the predator, but just as the paws reached him, there was a yelp and it fell to the forest floor. The other coyote was injured and ran back, but then turned on the sentry who had shot his pack mate, jumping at its face and killing him instantly, even as more shots rang out and it fell to the ground as well.

Suddenly, it was quiet. The whole thing was over in a

matter of minutes, and the ensuing silence was deafening. Only one of his guards remained, and he had a gash along his left arm that was bleeding freely. Five coyotes lay motionless on the ground, and Arnold was astounded that he, himself, was virtually untouched. He looked at the semiautomatics and picked one of them up.

The remaining guard moved to him menacingly and spoke. "No. No guns for you."

"Like hell." Arnold nodded at the two dead men. "I can't see them needing these anymore." He took a good look at the figure in front of him and softened. "Hey, you're bleeding. Do you have any bandages or first aid stuff in your pack?"

The guard dropped his knapsack to the ground. Arnold fished through it and found some gauze and wrapped the man's wounds. These automatons *had* saved his life. Darkness was setting in, but the scent of blood seemed to be everywhere. If he, a mere human, could smell it, surely there were other animals that could too. They needed to move on; he had the feeling he had not seen the last of angry predators.

CHAPTER 17

Russell was spending a lot of time with Teresa, pouring over equations and tables and stretching his genius mind in ways he had never imagined. And still the questions hovered at the edge of his awareness: How would they decide where to go? What if they got into space and the system didn't work? It was all just theory; it had never been tried. The nearest neighboring solar system was the binary star of Alpha Centauri and Proxima Centauri, which was over four light-years away, so that meant even at the speed of light, it would take over four years to get there. And wouldn't that be exactly where the GGP would aim for if they could? The last thing Russell wanted was to get his people off the Earth before she completely reclaimed herself, and away from Ganaffe and his following, only to have to fight them on some alien planet. He intended to bring weapons because it was irresponsible not to when going into such an unknown, but he sincerely hoped that no one would ever need to fire a single shot.

But if they could exceed the speed of light by two, three, four times, or more? It was still a long time to sustain more than two thousand people on a ship, fed and healthy. Not to mention, to keep them from killing each other after a while.

Structurally, he trusted Teresa's work. His knowledge of architectural design allowed him to make the connecting leaps when he saw what she had accomplished. He had already directed the contractors and engineers to begin making modifications to the spacecraft in its lair under a lip of the mountain. Troy DeJacob, Dr. Lister's partner, had dubbed the ship the *Phoenix*. There was no hiding the activity now, and many people were curious. It had become imperative that *no one* leave the compound, as they could be forced to give away these plans.

Teresa had shown Russell the design she and her husband had worked out to harness and contain gamma radiation for conversion to photovoltaic cells, which would provide for their energy needs, including light and climate control along with air circulation on board a ship the size of the *Phoenix*. They had basically created a new substance by applying a modified film of polycrystalline diamond and fusing it onto and within lead that was only an inch thick, producing a new form of insulation that they had named polymantine. It would reflect the very short gamma waves that otherwise could cut through six inches of lead like a knife through soft butter and so keep it from escaping its container. From there, it could be converted to electricity or to propulsion power to initiate the soliton or traditional thrusters. The new material wasn't that hard to produce, but it had taken an inordinate amount of ingenuity to develop.

Teresa and Devon were working feverishly on expanding the container and collecting gamma radiation and bringing the compound's two resident physicists, Morgan O'Keefe and Steven Seltzer, up to speed on the new technologies. Each scientist had found their way to the mountain oasis independently from different regions of the country, and both were certifiably brilliant. They could hardly contain their excitement over the research Teresa brought and had dived right in to assist in creating solutions to emerging problems.

There was a certain feeling of urgency. The Ramapo Fault line was not far away and had become more active in the last couple of years, partly due to the heightened tectonic movement out west. The increased vibration of the San Andreas was shaking up the whole continent, as far east as the Appalachians. Their geologist, Troy DeJacob, predicted that within the next year or two, even the Catskills could become too unstable to live on.

The weather patterns in the surrounding region had become more and more ominous, and the frequency with which they had to shutter the compound was increasing. It interfered with their harvest, their energy production, and their ability to spend time outdoors. The last few hours had delivered a fine ashen mist from forest fires in Utah burning out of control. There was virtually nothing left to burn in what was once California, where the lack of vegetation made mudslides uncontrollable, as the ground did not absorb the moisture when it rained. But as the fires moved closer to the East Coast, the fallout from the sky became more prevalent. Russell had every resident fitted with a respirator and face shield, and on days like this, the ash settled on the shields and obscured vision even further.

Braelyn walked into Russell's office, her face a cloud of dark emotion.

"Sahina Keter is gone," she said.

"What? Who's Sahina Keter?"

Braelyn gave him an incredulous look. "You *really* have been spending too much time with that Teresa. Have you forgotten about the rest of this place?"

Russell furrowed his brows for a moment. "Oh! The stray you brought in. I was going to go down and question him, but with everything else going on, I didn't get to it yet. What do you mean, 'he's gone'? I thought you had him locked away so he couldn't do any damage."

"I did. That's the thing. That door *was* deadbolted, and I had Aaron stationed outside of it, so if he needed something, you know. But when I went back down this morning, Aaron unlocked the door for me, and he was gone. The room was empty." Her face was nearly black with fury. "The deadbolt was still locked!"

"Was he hiding inside? Waiting until the door was opened so he could get away?"

"No. We searched it, and I swept it with my mind. There was no one in there. Aaron said he might have fallen asleep for a little bit, but the door was still deadbolted, so Sahina shouldn't have been able to get out anyway."

"Asleep? That's not appropriate. If he were tired, he should have called for someone to relieve him so he could rest."

Braelyn squinted at her brother. "What's kept you from interviewing him? You might have gotten further than I did. I can't read him, not at all. I can't even tell if he's a 'he' or a 'she!' He's hiding something important. I don't know how he's been able to shield himself from me, but I was hoping you could break through."

Russell put his hands over his face and rubbed his eyes. "There's been so much on my mind with these new discoveries… Where would he go? Did he come here to get intel and report back somewhere? If so, is he checking out the ship? Tampering with the food supply? Does he even know how to get out of here once he finishes whatever he's doing? And even if he is benign, if he exits and leaves a gate open…"

Russell put his hands down on the desk. "Find him, Brae. Whatever it takes. Engage all personnel. Talk to Ric, he combs the grounds daily, maybe he saw him. Put the word out. *Someone* has seen this guy. He's a stranger, he'll stand out. And make sure there have been no unauthorized eyes on the *Phoenix*!"

CHAPTER 18

Arnold wiped his hand across his face, trying to get the mist out of his eyes. It came away with a sliminess that made him take a better look in the falling light. It wasn't normal rain; it was dirty somehow. Like an emulsion. Although there was definitely moisture in whatever was falling, it was infused with grit and dust and made him want to seek cover immediately and wait it out. He located an overhang of rock to settle under and headed for it.

The remaining zombie guard moved with him and blocked his way. "We keep moving," it said.

"Hey, man—or whatever you are. This stuff isn't normal. It can't be good to breathe." The zombie stared, blank-faced. "Well, would you just look at it? Look what's on your clothes. We're breathing this. It could be poisonous!"

Slowly, as if in first gear, the guard turned to his shoulder and then his arm. He stared at the film that was growing there, like a layer of snow, except it was too brown and the temperature was only in the low fifties. Then he turned back toward the mountain and reached out for Arnold's arm to drag him along.

Arnold resisted and the zombie guard smacked him across the face. Then it took him by his shoulders, physically turned him toward the summit of the mountain, and gave him a hard push.

Arnold started forward reluctantly. He wasn't getting out of this. He realized suddenly that he had absolutely no idea what he was supposed to do when he got to his destination—wherever that was going to be. He assumed it had something to do with the imaginary oasis the resistance postulated. But with each step, that feeling of walking through cellophane became a little stronger. Or was that the mist falling from the sky?

He heard a far-off howl. It made him think of the snarling coyotes and then of the little girl and her kitten. For a fleeting second, he had doubts. I don't want to do this, he thought. I don't want to hurt anyone. Justine and her pack of cronies were far away and maybe Arnold could just leave. Ditch the guard and circle back to collect his family and then…just…run.

As he considered these thoughts, his head began to hurt. The more disloyal his thinking, the heavier his head felt. But it nagged at him. Why was it wrong to care about a little girl and her kitten? Every breath now felt like a knife going through him. He couldn't shake the image of the dead girl on the ground, bleeding from her belly and her last words: "Help Tiger."

Arnold glanced at the guard to see if it noticed the change in his attitude. But the blank-faced man just kept on trekking and, every once in a while, would give Arnold a shove to keep up the pace. Eventually, Arnold gave up and shut his mind down. The headache and pain in his chest went away immediately once he stopped fighting for his own thoughts.

They came to a small plateau, and Arnold, out of breath, demanded they stop for a minute. The rain was letting up but the fog, or whatever it was, remained. "What is this stuff?" he asked of the zombie, who never seemed to tire.

"Ashes."

"Ashes, like from fire?"

"Ashes."

Not a great conversationalist, Arnold thought. He peered through the mist but couldn't see more than a few feet ahead. He sat down at the edge of the clearing and rooted through the backpack looking for the granola bar he knew he had packed.

The guard stood still and stared straight ahead.

"What are you?" Arnold asked him but received no response. "I mean, you look and bleed like a human, but you act like...what did they *do* to you?"

"I am experimental intelligence."

Arnold nearly choked. "What does that mean? Your body appears human."

"My body is human, yes."

"What is 'experimental intelligence'?"

"My thinking has been modified to serve the Great Ganaffe. You are to follow the orders given, and I am here to make sure of that."

"Do you know what my orders are? Because I don't even know."

"You will know. They all always know, when it is time.

You were given orders, but you have not yet reached the trigger event, so they have not been activated."

Arnold wanted to sit and process that, but the zombie thing was done resting. "We go now. Enough sitting." It pulled Arnold up by the back of his hoodie, and they started uphill again.

CHAPTER 19

Russell walked into a lively discussion in the conference room. His geologist was there, Troy DeJacob, and was sitting next to Tobi Lister. Ricardo was present but looking out of his element, and Braelyn and Joshua, Teresa and Devon, Amira, and two other heads of department were seated around the table. Jennifer was their resident information technology expert; at twenty-seven, she could hack anything that a human could create, and she could write programs to do virtually anything at all. She and her colleague, Jason, were working on their new quantum computer which they had just powered up. The physicists, Morgan O'Keefe and Steven Seltzer, were sitting huddled together near Teresa, still pondering equations.

There was a coffee maker on a table off to the side of the room which had been nearly emptied, and Russell poured himself the last cup. The room mostly quieted when Russell took a seat. He surprised himself with how grim he sounded.

"We are going to have to make some tough decisions very soon." He looked around the table; he had everyone's complete attention. He continued as matter-of-factly as he could.

"*Where* are we going? *When* are we going? *Who* is going? *What* are we taking? And…what and who are we leaving behind"

The room was silent. Accustomed to awkward pauses since his childhood, Russell just waited.

It was Jennifer who broke the silence. "I don't understand. I thought we were all staying together. Here, and then wherever we end up."

Russell sighed, but Morgan stepped in. "We built a ship. The *Phoenix* was originally intended to send a small number of us out to look for another world, while the bulk would need to stay here. We assumed it would take years to get anywhere, so most never dreamed they would be actually traveling into space. And the time factor made it unlikely that we could bring enough supplies for a significant number of us to survive the long journey it would take to get anywhere we could potentially land. I mean, we have to stock enough food on that ship for everyone to eat for the duration of the journey. Yes, we have space for a botanical garden, but…we could quite possibly starve to death."

"Right. So something has changed?" Jennifer asked.

"Indeed," Steven said. "Everything has changed. If these equations translate accurately, which it appears they should, we *could* make it to a neighboring solar system in a matter of months. Maybe weeks. That means, we could conceivably take a *lot* more of us—"

"But not *all* of us," Amira broke in. "Is that what you're saying?"

Steven frowned. "The ship just isn't large enough to carry twenty-five hundred people. I mean, unless we rebuild it from the ground up. And I don't see us having time, according to Troy." He turned to acknowledge Troy, who was nodding sadly. "And also," Steven continued, "the bigger the ship, the greater the mass, and while mass is meaningless at the speed of light, we need the thruster capacity to break out of orbit and initiate that velocity. Even if we use a soliton." He looked sheepish and uncomfortable.

"How many can we take, and how do we choose?" Braelyn asked.

"The ship was designed to accommodate a large number for a long trip, so there is a fair amount of space. A gym area, relatively spacious lodgings, an observation deck, a few places to just walk and get exercise," Morgan explained. "We can do some reconstruction on the inside to accommodate more living quarters. It would be a bit of a squeeze, but if it was only for a few weeks or months, it would certainly be livable."

"So, *how many* can we fit?" Dr. Lister asked.

The two physicists looked at each other and then averted their eyes.

Teresa spoke up. "The ship you have designed is beautifully constructed and, with a few modifications that we are working on presently, it is well suited for faster-than-light travel. It can, as you said, be redesigned internally to increase living space, and if people will consent to three or four to a room for the relatively short period of time, it should accommodate about fifteen hundred travelers."

A minute passed, and then another. No one spoke. The implications of that were staggering. So many escapees were possible—if they were willing to take the risk. And so many must be left behind. Alone, on a planet that was becoming uninhabitable, in a country whose government was obsessed with cruelty.

The United States was not the only country in this predicament. Right-wing fanatics had grabbed power in nearly every previously free, democratic part of the world, so no place was safe anymore. And of course, the planetary changes were happening everywhere. Many parts of Africa had suffered so many earthquakes and volcanoes that even the cooler regions were crumbling. The Antarctic and North poles were mostly melted, and the water tables had risen so that Japan, the Philippine Islands, and much of Greece were now underwater, and new beachfront property had emerged in coastal areas around the world.

Russell folded his fingers together and put his hands in front of him on the table. "We will need to come up with a means to choose. First, we have to know how many are interested in the journey. If there are fifteen hundred or less, no problem, but…"

Troy nodded his head with his lips pursed. "It's simple, really. The young people go. To survive on a new world, to make it our home, we will need to build a society and that means we need numbers. We need children, and people of childbearing age, and people strong enough to endure unpredictable circumstances." He looked up. "Face the facts. Not everyone will survive. Our strength will be in our numbers. Those of us," he said, looking at Tobi, "who are older, we're not going to live that many more years anyway."

Troy and Tobi were both over sixty-five, and while they looked younger, it was an inarguable fact. Even Russell was in his late fifties and Braelyn had just passed sixty. Although the siblings, perhaps owing to the drugs they had been subjected to as small children, seemed to age more slowly than would be considered normal.

Ricardo piped up, "Well, that would include half of the skilled people here. I have no wish to go off into the wilderness with no doctor, or land on an unknown planet with no geologist or meteorologist, and no one with tried and true leadership skills. It can't *just* be about age." He looked straight at Russell. "I'm sorry, dude, but you took us this far; don't think you're going to abandon us on the most momentous journey of humankind. I'm serious."

Everyone started talking at once, with a mixture of fear, excitement, and confusion rising out of the cacophony. Finally, Russell stood up and raised both hands, like stop signs.

"Easy, everyone, please. Nothing is being decided today. We all need to think long and hard about this. Every one of you here is an essential linchpin in our little society, and I want to hear from each of you—after you've had time to consider it carefully. I'd like to reconvene in forty-eight hours for further discussion. Please, please do not speak of this outside our group yet, except to your families for their opinions. No one will be expected to leave loved ones behind. But swear them to secrecy for the moment. I don't want a panic before we have a chance to present to the community at large, which will likely be in the next week."

Everyone started gathering their coffee cups to wash and headed for the door.

Braelyn called over the noise, "Hey, wait up. Has anyone seen the stranger, Sahina Keter? The guy who was hanging out near the tunnel entrance when we retrieved Teresa and Devon? We had to take him in with us, just so he couldn't give us away. But he was locked in a room on level three and now he's gone."

At another time, this might have evoked more concern, but there was a lot of headshaking as the group moved out.

Joshua came over to join his mother. "I think I did," he said.

"Where, and when?" Braelyn asked him. "Why didn't you tell anyone!"

Joshua shrugged. "I asked him if he was supposed to be here, and he said yes. It was in the valley. He was walking through the corn crop."

"When was that, Josh?" Russell took him by the shoulders.

Joshua scrunched up his eyes, trying to remember. "Maybe a couple of days ago?"

Russell grabbed Ricardo by the arm just as he was heading out the door. "Check the corn, Ric. Test it. Make sure it hasn't been tampered with. In fact, test everything. I want that man found ASAP!"

Ricardo nodded and left. Braelyn looked at Russell. "You know the news of the ship will be all over the community by nightfall."

"I know." Russell sighed. "And in the ears of Sahina Keter as well."

CHAPTER 20

Arnold was tired and thirsty. They had been walking for nearly twenty hours with minimal breaks. The zombie guard did not seem to fatigue. If he hadn't bled from the coyote bite, Arnold would have thought he was not just an intelligence experiment but a cyborg of sorts as well.

A mountain slope rose up before them. It was incredibly steep, and the side of the mountain under some brush was slick and smooth. There seemed no place for a hand or foot to find purchase. He soon realized the brush appeared to be there more for camouflage and didn't seem quite natural.

Arnold's heart beat faster. Was this it? Had he just found it? "Hey, no-name," he called out. Since the zombie thing wouldn't give his name, Arnold had settled on that. Better than calling him *it*. "What'ya think of this? Huh?"

The guard shuffled over slowly. It put its hand over the rock face but said nothing.

———

In the security room deep within the mountain, a piercing alarm went off. Erika ran to the console and muted it, but it still showed throughout the complex as a flashing red light. She checked all the cameras individually and settled on a single image of two male figures standing at the periphery of the south end. It seemed the only site of concern. There was something odd about one of them, but both were definitely testing the surface of the mountain that separated the compound from the chaos of the outside world.

She spoke in rapid bites into the comm and alerted Russell, Ricardo, and Angelo, who was the security chief of arms. Angelo was the slowest to respond—it had been at least a year since he had been called up, and the alert took him completely by surprise. He sent for eight of his core people, and they donned helmets and Kevlar vests, semiautomatics, and tasers. It was always preferable to capture intruders alive for questioning, but they didn't take any chances.

In truth, they used to get these alarms not infrequently, as members of the resistance would find their way to the mountainside and plead for admission. They took in a lot of people then, not all vetted as well as Angelo would have liked. Braelyn seemed to pass judgment on them with her "gut feelings" and Angelo didn't trust that. For all he knew, they could already have multiple spies living on the grounds, poised and ready to sabotage anything they chose. But it was not Angelo's place to question either of the Vaderman siblings. He was grateful that he had been able to come here with his family and live in relative peace.

Angelo had been in the National Guard and then in the Chicago Police Department, but in the last five years, anyone who wasn't squeaky clean White was denigrated, and he began to fear for his family. He and his best friend had heard about this place, and they had packed up their stuff in the middle of the night and headed out with Angelo's wife and two children, then ten and four. His friend had been killed on the journey by a gang of Marauders, for which Angelo still felt a burning need for vengeance when he gave it leave to fill him up. Generally, he tried to squash it from his conscious mind.

Now that the kids were fifteen and nine, Angelo saw every passing year they survived as a movement forward toward the time when they might actually be able to defend themselves and be less likely to fall prey to the Whispies and extremists. In addition to their academic lessons, he had them train daily in martial arts and strength building to lessen their vulnerability, and his wife trained with them. His daughter, Tennessee, was even fiercer than her older brother.

Angelo nodded to his armed contingent, and they headed for the bulwark at the south end. There was no entrance at the rock face where the outsiders had been spotted, but he sent four to the gates on each side of where they had been seen and checked in with Erika by radio to see if there had been any movement or other threats revealed.

Erika told him the potential intruders were moving east along the ridge, and every few steps, were checking for purchase into the mountainside. It was not typical resistance behavior. Usually, those seeking sanctuary looked desperate and tried to signal with their arms while looking over their shoulders, hoping someone would see them and let them in.

Erika's account that they were moving so purposefully sounded like this was truly a security threat.

———

Arnold felt excitement as he moved around the rock face. There was something unusual about this mountain. Something unnatural. He *felt* it. This was the place! But how to get inside? And stay unnoticed. All the doubts he had been feeling and the visions of the little girl and her kitten were miles and miles away. When he looked down, the Earth appeared softer somehow, as if filtered through cellophane, and Arnold's head was almost painfully focused on the task at hand. *Find the place. Enter the place. Transmit the coordinates. If caught, take the little pill in your pocket.*

His mission. Why hadn't he remembered it until now? It was crystal clear. He did not seem to care about the unanswered questions around what to do if discovered, or what the "little pill" was. Something ominous pulled at his mind when he thought about taking some unknown pill if he were seen, but he set it aside for the task at hand. No doubt he was born for this mission. He must not fail. He would not fail.

He glanced at no-name shuffling beside him. The thing wasn't being terribly helpful. It wasn't looking for clues in the Earth or offering any suggestions. But it was holding some small apparatus and pointing it at the mountain.

"What is that?" Arnold asked.

"Heat seeker."

"What?" Arnold walked over and looked at the screen. It took his eyes some time to adjust and then to realize what he was looking at. It was measuring infrared, but it seemed to be doing its inspection right through the rock. As they continued gradually around the mountain, Arnold noticed a subtle decrease in density in one region and—yes! There were infrared shadows approaching from there, as if it were a tunnel of sorts.

Arnold ran to the exact place where the density was least and stood as if ready to open a door. He didn't even pull out the gun he had retrieved. It was like he wanted to greet an old friend rather than invade a secret hideaway. His head felt dizzy, and while a distant part of him was valiantly trying to put the brakes on, he ran right up to the mountainside and started banging on it and yelling almost cheerfully.

"Hey, let me in!"

———

In the vestibule inside the mountain, Angelo and three of his crew stood with weapons raised and watched the scene on the other side of the gateway from the camera feed. Some maniac was now pounding on the door.

Russell walked up behind Angelo so quietly that Angelo hadn't realized he'd arrived.

"Something's wrong with that man," Russell whispered.

Angelo jumped. "No shit, Sherlock, he looks like he's taken a happy pill."

"No, the other man. The one just standing there. He barely moves a muscle, but he's not crouching like he's trying to hide." Russell peered more closely at the camera. "It's almost like he's unconscious."

As they watched the camera, the strange man who barely seemed to breathe took a device of sorts out of his pocket. He pushed a button initiating a faint yellow light on its console and held it up above his head.

Almost as one, Russell and Angelo reacted. "Get down!"

There was a blast, and the pack the strange man was wearing blew up, sending shrapnel flying. Both men outside were killed instantly.

The mountainside was untouched. Except for a small brush fire to the local greenery, there was no structural damage to anything. Angelo wanted to go put out the fire, but Russell raised a finger to wait.

"What was the purpose of that? It was a suicide mission. Unless it was to get us to open up and let in a larger faction."

They waited while Erika did a thorough sweep with her cameras. They sent out two bird-shaped drones to look for other would-be intruders, but none were found.

"It doesn't make any sense," Russell said on the radio to Erika, just as he found Amira by his side.

"Russell, we need to look at what's out there and clear it away regardless. And there may also be clues on the ground."

"How did they find us?" Russell asked her.

"Let's go see." Amira led the way out. She carefully went through the contents of what had been an extremely ineffectual bomb, noting that it was certainly not designed to hurt their stronghold significantly or even to create a path to break in. It *was* designed to eliminate the agents of this operation. On closer examination, Amira found and identified the remains of the infrared sensor.

"This. This is how they found the entrance." She held it up. "It measures heat and density. Just point it at the walls and keep moving until it penetrates—when it's working, that is. Now it's scrap, of course."

"This mountainside is solid rock for six hundred feet except for the narrow tunnel; they must have known the explosive would be insufficient," Angelo said. "So what was the detonation for, just a distraction? A warning? They killed themselves. For what purpose? There's nothing else out here."

But Amira was not answering. Something else had caught her eye. Something that had been shallowly dug into the Earth and displaced by the explosion. It looked like it was still functional, as a faint blue light pulsed inside it.

"That."

Russell walked alongside her. "Another bomb?"

"Doubtful. We have seen no other activity around the compound," Amira said and looked up at Russell. "I think it is a transmitter."

"Oh my God," Russell said. "The door. If the explosion didn't show up on their radar—"

"The transmitter will," Amira finished.

"Step back," Russell said, and he took sharp aim at the transmitter with his semiautomatic.

"Wait!" Amira stepped quickly in front of him. "Bring it somewhere else before you destroy it. Let it transmit a different set of coordinates. Maybe it will confuse them for a while."

One of Angelo's men volunteered to take it to a neighboring ridge. He set off on horseback to avoid using any traceable technology and took with him a small timed explosive device. Russell instructed him to reenter through a different gate. It might give them a few extra hours, maybe a day, but the damage was done. They were discovered.

CHAPTER 21

The control center in the compound was abuzz with activity. The red alerts had been noted throughout the encampment, and all the residents were on edge. As per protocol, everyone spoke in whispered tones and stayed within the mountain. No music played and no machinery was in operation. At three hours post event, there was still no sign of any prying eyes, whether in the skies or by land. There was also still no sign of Sahina Keter.

In urgent, hushed tones, Teresa and Devon huddled with the *Phoenix* team, looking at potential galaxies and hedging their bets on which star was most likely to have an Earth analog—a planet sufficiently Earthlike to sustain life.

The new planet most likely needed to be orbiting a sun of roughly the same age as their own Sol. Sol is a G2 star, meaning a yellow dwarf, which is fairly young in astronomical terms, and gives off a great amount of heat and energy. That energy is necessary to provide water in its liquid form, which in turn could support plant life and photosynthesis, essential foundations to providing oxygen and creating a biosphere that could sustain mammalian life.

Joshua had wandered in and started asking questions. "Why are all these planets named Kepler with numbers after them? Are they all in the same place?"

Steve Seltzer had a doctorate in physics and loved teaching, but this hardly seemed to be the time. He turned to Joshua, obviously about to dismiss him.

"Wait," Teresa said, "if Josh has questions, others will too." She turned to Joshua. "A long time ago, NASA sent a telescope out into space to make recordings for us. That telescope was called Kepler. So every star that it recorded was given the name Kepler with a number after it, designating the order in which they were discovered, and planets orbiting that star were given additional letters."

Joshua nodded and backed away a little bit, looking embarrassed by having been nearly censored for his curiosity.

Morgan's field was both electromagnetism and astrophysics. She laid out celestial maps onto a long table. The mood was solemn. They had never studied these things with the real possibility of going there; in the past, it was always just a wistful idea.

"These two systems seem most likely. Kepler 442b, in the constellation Lyra. It's twelve hundred light years away and its sun is an orange dwarf. Its orbit around its star is one hundred twelve days—"

Steve broke in, "But an orange dwarf may not be hot enough."

"True, but its distance from its sun is half that of Earth to

Sol. So this planet may be in the Goldilocks Zone for that system. Observations suggest a rocky core."

"Other possibilities?"

Morgan pointed to another star system, this time in the Cygnus constellation. "Kepler 452b. Its sun is a yellow dwarf, about six billion years old, so older than our sun, but only by one and a half billion years," she smiled, "and nearly the same temperature and mass. There's a better than even chance it will have a rocky surface."

Joshua was bursting with questions. "Why do we want it to be rocky? Wouldn't it be nicer if it had soil and things to plant stuff in?"

Even Steve laughed. "Of course, Joshua, but plants can't grow on the surface if the planet is mostly gas, like Jupiter and Saturn are. The soil and plants need the rock underneath to give them a stable surface to grow on. Also, we'll need to build shelters, places to live." He turned back to the group. "Its orbit is three hundred eight-five days, similar to Earth, and it's fourteen hundred light years away. The difference in distances to these two planets is not that significant if we are using a soliton warp drive. And if we are not…" he shrugged, "then we aren't going anywhere anyway."

"Is that a wrap on our options?" Jason asked.

"Last one." Morgan pulled another stellar map up onto the screen they were using. "Kepler 186, just outside the Cygnus system but adjacent to it. It is the closest to us, a mere 492.5 light years away." She smirked. "The star is a red dwarf, so it's older and much cooler than the others and cooler than our Earth's sun, but there does seem to be promising conditions on the fifth planet in its orbit, 186f. This planet's year is one hundred thirty days. The advantage is its relative proximity. I mean, compared to the others."

"What color will the sky be if the sun is orange or red instead of yellow?" Jason asked. "Just curious."

"That depends on the gases in the atmosphere much more than the color of the sun, but the cooler the star, the less light overall. From the surface of the planet, the sun may appear close to white, just like ours does, but with a faint reddish hue, and the atmosphere will reflect the composition of its gases."

"Are we really doing this?" Jennifer nearly whispered.

Teresa laughed, the first anyone had seen her do so. "Only if that quantum computer of yours is completely functional!"

The team threw around other choices, including the binary system of Alpha Centauri and Proxima Centauri, but concluded that if they could develop a warp drive, then the GGP could at some point as well, and would likely set out for the nearest solar system. No one bothered to suggest that in deep space, differences among humans *should* be easily put aside and the fact of being of the same race in a vast universe of aliens would bind them together.

The GGP did not see the human race as one people.

Over the years, it had become increasingly obvious that the population that followed Ganaffe was drugged on a continuous basis. Scopolamine in their food and water primed them and then the GGP reinforced their objectives using language specifically targeted at misrepresenting daily existence. Social media and the television networks were entirely controlled by the GGP and maintained the deceptions.

But even with minimal use of the drug, it was becoming

possible to persuade almost anyone to do just about anything, as long as it was presented in terms of long forgotten, but revered values. The GGP would compare following their party line as akin to loyalty and said that people of integrity and compassion would see it as the highest form of existence. They showed video clips of Asians and African Americans being executed *en masse* and called it "purification" of the population. Even Caucasians were being slaughtered if they were "polluting" the environment with dangerous, independent thinking. It was all for the "Greater Good," and it was only broadcast within the country and to other countries that had newly adopted similar radical right wing practices.

The Ganaffe regime had begun to send squadrons of scouts out into space, men who had been preconditioned to become slaves in whatever world they settled on. Teresa knew directly of the legion that had been sent to Enceladus, Jupiter's moon, but she had heard rumor that other divisions were being sent elsewhere, while the GGP waited to hear back from whoever had survived and found a viable planet to occupy. It was this that led to an attitude that lacked concern for preservation of the Earth, and threw all caution to the wind instead of seeking to protect what might be salvageable. By appeasing their mass's addiction to a free reign of chaos, the GGP imposed a fierce psychological hold over them.

The team continued in heated debate for hours until they determined they were ready to present the results to Russell.

They called him down for a full report, and there was a mood of blistering excitement and fear as they presented their findings and recommendations. It was Russell who had developed this oasis on land that had been his own Catskills' property and Russell who had received some bizarre, spiritual guidance back in 2020 by which his little summer estate had blossomed into an entire compound, replete with state-of-the-art surveillance systems, weapons, and stealth equipment. Russell had funded the entire operation, and so it was Russell who would make the ultimate decision. No one even questioned it.

The truth was, Russell was instructed to purchase these items and somehow the money to do so had started appearing in his accounts. He had already been a multimillionaire from his unparalleled work as an architect, but his net worth seemed to rise exponentially without connection to the activity of the stock markets or his having completed any recent projects. When the enigmatic man named Harris had left him, he told Russell that there would be need of these defenses, and that they would be supplied to him with the expectation that Russell would provide sanctuary to deserving souls.

Russell had done his best to comply, but it was a tremendous responsibility and even a burden to feel that his decision about going off-world could mean the survival or death of his entire little community, and possibly, humanity at large. The fact that they had to leave about half behind weighed heavily on him. He prayed that there would be room for all those who wanted to come. And that the little haven would continue on without him, as well protected as it had been thus far.

In twelve years, no one affiliated with the GGP had stumbled upon them, by chance or by intention. Russell was quite sure that was not an accident, and when he would let his mind go supremely quiet, he thought he could still sense *El Curandero Grande*, the shaman from his past, hovering just out of reach and weaving a web of protection. But it had been so long since he'd had any contact with the ancient man with the paper-thin skin and the long white beard. He was probably just imagining it.

While most of the residents of the compound saw it as Russell having opened up his home, some knew that, to Russell, he had merely been a conduit for some higher-powered destiny. He had shared with a select few that he was told by the ancient shaman there were always a handful of individuals chosen in each generation for the possibility of great need, and that he had been "activated." So far, Russell didn't feel he had made any significant contribution outside of the compound itself, which had somehow grown to fifty times its original size, but that was fine by him.

Russell was also intensely lonely. Losing his wife five years ago had taken a toll, even though they had never really resonated intellectually, and Russell had become wary of her when her sensitivity to being drugged by scopolamine had deeply affected their lives together. He still felt guilt over not having been able to protect her—not anticipating that she would be used in the way she was. If he had spent more time teaching her, if he had better impressed upon her the dangers of going out and had kept her home, and safe…

Now Russell's heart could never be stirred again other than by someone whose intellect was equivalent to his own, someone who was savvy to what was happening on the planet. And in this closed society, who was there to meet? He found himself perpetually alone with his aloneness.

Teresa cocked her head sideways at Russell and prompted him. "Are you following us?"

Russell shook his head. "I'm sorry. I'm just... Yes, I'm following. So you recommend Kepler 186f, in the Cygnus constellation, because it's the closest, and cuts our travel time by half. But it also has the coolest sun. What do you predict are our chances of making it? Plotting the course, managing the warp, and the likelihood it will in fact be a planet we can inhabit?"

Jennifer answered, "We are about as ready as we will ever be. I've programmed Dr. Simmons's equations into the quantum computer, and it's ready to go. I've also entered the coordinates of the other two stars in case we have to change course along the way. As for the likelihood that any of these will be a viable home...that's going to be a risk wherever we shoot for."

CHAPTER 22

ussell returned to his rooms by himself. Everyone had limited space. Either a large, divided room serving as a bedroom/living area with a small table off to the side to eat and a desk for work or a large studio-type apartment, with much the same features except that there was no separation of sleeping and living room areas. Families with children had an extra room, and those children between twelve and eighteen could move into a dormitory if they chose. Space had become rationed as their population grew in size. He marveled to himself that he had lived here for the last twelve years. When it began, he thought it would be temporary, a year at most, until the pandemics of coronavirus and hatred had both faded away.

He sat in his favorite chair, one he had brought from his Midtown Manhattan apartment, and put some solo piano music on ever so softly. He missed his piano; he was a talented pianist in his own right, but it had not been expedient to bring it in the beginning. He always thought he would go back for it, but that became impractical amid the rapidly mounting violence in the city. He closed his eyes and let memories wash over him.

The little boy of three, holed up in the mountains in the Peruvian Andes with his big sister, while their mother received some ritualistic healing for her autoimmune disease, wandering (or summoned?) into the sacred shaman's hut. How was he to know it was supposed to be forbidden? As if he were back there once again, his breath seemed to contain the smoke of the incense that had nearly choked him, the haze so thick it obscured everything but those white, blind but all-seeing eyes that penetrated through the mist and looked directly into little Russell's soul. He felt again the pull, wanting to leave but unable to move, and sensed the shaman speaking directly into his mind.

> *You are gifted, young child. You will be blessed.*
> *Your mind shall have no limit; no door shall remain closed*
> *to you.*
> *You shall be a* Curandero Grande, *even as I am.*
> *You will see into the hearts of others, and you will enter*
> *their souls at will.*
> *The Spirits have foreseen your coming, and today I make*
> *it so.*
> *When next the Holy Plants find you, all doors will open…*

Russell had never been particularly religious or interested in paranormal phenomena. His mind was so active, it was all he could do to keep facts organized, and he avoided anything that required a leap. Yet he also understood that reason alone could never account for the myriad of experiences and irrational events that had unequivocally occurred. The quantum theory he had studied and the warp drive they were developing more and more made it seem like many aspects of science and theology were one.

Russell sat straight in his chair and deliberately relaxed every muscle in his body, starting with his facial muscles and continuing to his toes. His breath was deep and even, and by sheer force of will, he quieted the chatter of his thoughts.

He let his mind hover and then soar. He sought the shaman; pictured him in his head, reached for him. In twelve years, the mysterious force that had awakened and then saved him had gone dark, but Russell was in dire need of guidance now. They were all looking to him to determine where to go. Even, if they *should* go.

His mind drifted, concentrating on a state of lack of focus. He imagined the countryside below him, then the state of New York, and then the whole eastern seaboard, with much of the former coast underwater. Long Island had shrunk to a fraction of its former size, while Hilton Head and most of Cape Cod were completely submerged; Bermuda was no longer visible, either. The pictures came at him as if through no effort of his own. As his mind's eye rose higher, he saw the United States, with fires raging out west, and desert where once forest existed. The great blemish where the Rocky Mountains now jutted higher than ever and seemed to have pushed the land eastward, like a wound in the planet's crust, and the Pacific Ocean encroached upon the continent from the west. Finally, all of North America and then south, into Northern Peru.

He saw *El Curandero Grande's* hut. Still in the clearing on the forest floor, surrounded by tall trees, the air heavy with moisture, all foggy and gray. Russell was sure he was just projecting a memory from long ago, but he pushed on. Searching, seeking…

And suddenly the ancient man was there, stroking his white beard, and nodding, as if it had been yesterday when last they met.

Welcome, my child.

Russell tried to settle on the ground next to him, but his mind seemed to be pulled by some astral wind, until the old man reached out and gently pulled him to the Earth, tethering him there, as if he might spiral off again in a moment.

Russell found himself nearly breathless. "I need help," he said.

The ancient apparition just nodded again and waited.

"This is too much. I cannot do this alone. I don't know where to go. I don't know *if* we should go. I don't want to be responsible…"

The shaman passed his hand between them, as if wiping away Russell's mental frenzy.

You are not alone. You have never been alone.

"But what do I do?" Russell felt like he was becoming hysterical.

What does your heart tell you?

Russell stopped. He had been looking outward for some logical answer. Now he turned inward.

"It says we will die if we stay here."

Then you must go.

"But where? There are several planets, all just *possibilities* of survival; how do I choose? Which is the right one? How will I know?"

All choices are right. All choices are wrong. Each has its challenges. It depends on what you do when you get there.

Russell was quiet. He could hardly look at the shaman, and he could not quite look away.

"They found us, you know. They're coming for us."

The shaman just looked at him—looked *into* him.

"How much time do we have? We are not ready…"

No one is ever ready for big change. But you always have what you need. You must begin in order to get there.

Russell did not find that especially helpful. "What of you? The planet is… it's breaking up. You will die here. Do you… do you want to come? *Can* you come with us? Would you?"

Do not concern yourself with me. You must go now. You have much to do.

"But—but I need you to be with me."

I am, and have always been, with you, my son. To find me, you must only look…

The visage faded away, and suddenly the anchor that had held him dissolved and Russell found himself swirling in a smaze with no point of reference. He nearly panicked again. He had to get back home; he didn't feel solid. He had a fleeting vision of Teresa and her quiet strength, and it sent him careening forward and after a breathless minute, he was back in his little apartment, and the spinning sensation faded away. Nausea rose in his gullet, but he stood up and started walking around the room, needing to feel the ground beneath his feet, needing to know the world was solid once more. Was that what they called "astral projection?"

His head cleared slowly, and he became aware that his intercom was buzzing frantically.

"Yeah," Russell nearly croaked. It was Angelo.

"Mr. Vaderman! We've picked up low-flying aircraft approaching from the south."

CHAPTER 23

Russell rushed down to the command center deep in the mountain. Sure enough, four blips on the radar screen were drawing steadily closer on a direct course to their coordinates. Angelo boosted detection of the radar signature, and the computer identified the craft by their radar cross sections, which illuminated the missiles they carried. They were bombers.

"Maybe they won't recognize us as their target," offered a young man at the console whom Russell had never met. "We do blend in pretty well."

"The GGP don't care if they destroy the wrong target," Angelo snapped back.

"They will if they are carrying a specific payload that is calculated for our destruction. They're ruthless and stupid, but if they go back and say they squandered their ammo on the wrong place, someone is going to be pretty pissed off, and that will not bode well for them," the man said. For a kid, he seemed pretty savvy. And very angry.

"What's your name?" Russell asked.

"Jimmy."

"You have some experience with these people."

Jimmy didn't answer. He pursed his lips into a tight line and consulted the computer system again. "Hey! There's someone in the middle of the valley. Is that a radio? What the hell is he doing?" Jimmy switched the compound's cameras to a large screen, and they all clearly saw a lone, slight figure in the middle of the cornfield operating a device that was set up on some sort of tripod. It was aimed at the southern sky. "It's like he's calling them right to us!"

"What the—" Angelo enhanced the image, and they saw a person in a dark blue, hooded sweatshirt, about five foot eight, with shoulder length brown hair tied back in a ponytail. There was a fierce energy about him as he worked fervently with his device.

Russell jumped up. "I'm going out there," he said. "Get a squad together."

"Mr. Vaderman, wait." Angelo ran to a cabinet and pulled out a couple of Kevlar suits, radios, and a gas mask and then handed Russell a semiautomatic. "I'm going with you."

"No, you're not. I can't spare you in here, and I can't risk you out there." He grabbed a radio. "Keep in touch."

"I'll go." No one had noticed Amira slip into the command center. She had a way of appearing suddenly in places, perhaps back to her days in the Mossad, when secrecy was often all that guaranteed survival. She grabbed the other set of gear and another weapon, and they left together.

Angelo called after them. "Contact with the planes in T minus seven minutes."

"Arm our antiaircraft missiles," Russell ordered, and felt a chill run up his spine. "Do not fire unless those planes come within fifteen hundred meters."

Long ago, the man named Harris, a.k.a. Horatius Marsden, had secured their high-tech defense system for what was at the time simply Russell's summer home here in the Catskills. He had not thought he would ever need it and had been reluctant to accept. So far, they had never needed to even consider using it, but Angelo did have someone perform a systems check every month to make sure everything remained in operational order. The thought of shooting planes out of the sky... Russell shuddered. But if it came down to us or them? There was also the understanding that once they did something like that, they would declare their presence. Their exact position, their capabilities. It was a measure to buy time, that was all. They could not hope to win in the long run.

Russell and Amira stepped cautiously outside into the valley. The Kevlar was in the colors of the local foliage, much as the floor of their little valley, so they blended in reasonably well, but still they crouched. Amira met his eyes and pointed in the direction of where the man had last been seen. They moved quickly but quietly.

"The planes have veered off slightly to the west," Angelo's voice in Russell's earpiece reported. "Still coming in hot. It may be their intention to strike us from the side, or they may be doing a first pass to evaluate."

"Are we ready to shoot them down?" Russell's voice was a whisper.

"Yes, sir. And we have secured the *Phoenix*. We can activate her own shields if needed—but that may cause her to show up on their radar. While it could just confuse them, it will definitely pique their curiosity."

"Stand ready to activate *Phoenix* shield," Russell said. They could *not* lose the *Phoenix*, no matter what. "How far are we from launch, if it comes to that?"

"Jennifer here. We could launch in as little as a day, but we still don't know who our passengers are or exactly where we're going."

"Copy," Russell whispered. "Get her prepped."

Amira tapped him on the shoulder and waved her finger ahead twice. A man was standing between the rows of corn. He was aiming something that resembled a telescope at the sky—not the direction the planes were coming from and not the mountainside, but somewhere off to the west. He appeared to be straining a bit. He glanced over his shoulder as Russell and Amira approached, and Amira signaled Russell to move to the right while she moved to the left, so that they would flank him.

The man sent a last burst of whatever he was transmitting, looked back in their direction, then dropped his instrument and ran off at lightning speed. Three seconds later, Russell and Amira converged at the device he had been using and searched rapidly for a way to shut it down. Except that it appeared to be already off. Amira ran after the trespasser and Russell wanted to shout to her, but she was gone.

His earpiece crackled. "Mr. Vaderman, the planes have turned, they're heading west. Confirm, the planes are heading west. They will miss us." Angelo's voice, filled with relief, was both welcome and puzzling. How did this happen? They had to have been seen. The planes were right here.

They sent a party out to meet up with Amira and search the grounds and Russell picked up the gadget. Amira told Russell through her radio comm that the man had appeared to her to be none other than Sahina Keter, but all signs of him had vanished. Nevertheless, she was continuing to search.

Back in the command center, Russell gave Keter's device to one of his engineers to analyze and instructed everyone to prepare for a community meeting that evening; he asked that his advisers arrive one hour early. Then he headed to the *Phoenix* to oversee preparations, rubbing his temples with his hands so hard, it was as if he wanted to erase his current reality.

He found Teresa, Devon, and Jennifer on the bridge of the ship, programming the quantum computer. It was larger than Russell had imagined and yet, considering what the Q could do, he supposed it wasn't very large at all.

It was bolted to the ceiling on the port side of the bridge. The system itself was spherical, and about the size of a basketball. It looked almost like a chandelier, with copper qubits hanging down from a superconducting chip, arranged a little like a chessboard. Its immediate environment was kept vacuum sealed, with the inside concentration of particulate matter even less than what is found in outer space. The encasement was made from Teresa's newly developed polymantine, which shrouded and protected it, increasing the size of the entire apparatus by twice. Polymantine was now the hardest substance known.

The Q operated at one hundred million times the speed of the fastest standard computer. It could calculate trajectories for the *Phoenix* in a fraction of an instant and program the soliton warp to precisely deliver them to orbit their destination. It could also calculate atmospheric composition on the surface of a planet and land them safely on any terrain that had a reasonably dense surface.

Russell stared at the machine, shimmering beneath the polymantine surface. It was a thing of beauty, and yet, it looked entirely alien. As he stood gazing at it, Ricardo buzzed in to say another severe storm was surging.

CHAPTER 24

Winds kicked up to 80 mph within a few minutes, and as if the Earth were in cahoots with the sky, there was an underground rumbling that seemed to mirror the thundering above. The Ramapo Fault shuddered with a 4.9 Richter scale event even as lightning struck the trees just outside the compound and the wind continued to gust faster.

Even before Russell gave the orders, Ricardo had the solar panels closed and covered, and everything went into lockdown as the sky darkened ominously. Angelo had been watching the radar and reported that the four planes seemed to have disappeared. They might even have crashed. What had sent them off course to begin with was a complete mystery, but they had been heading directly into what was now looking to be a bomb cyclone that had appeared out of nowhere, and there was a good chance the planes wouldn't make it back to their base to report their failure. So perhaps the weather *was* on their side.

Plans to have a town hall meeting had to be pushed back. Russell had to weigh the risks from the sky, where the wind was escalating steadily, with the risks of increasing seismic tremors that could conceivably cause the walls to collapse and trap them all underground. They had not yet seen a Ramapo quake measure higher than 4.5, but this was already greater. While this magnitude would do little above ground but cause a shudder in buildings, underground was a different story, and it was unnerving to be within the rock as it trembled.

Seismic activity greater than 9.5 had not been known anywhere until four years ago, when an earthquake in Southern California with a rating of 11.6 had literally reshaped the United States as far as the Sierra Nevada Mountains. The Hoover Dam had collapsed, causing overflow of the Colorado River banks all the way into Mexico. The land became more and more unstable after that, and within a year, the Rockies had shifted so that the terrain was unrecognizable to anyone who had flown over the skies previously. The increasing wildfires were unreachable, and now no one even pretended to try to put them out; the entire West Coast had become a graveyard.

It was, of course, not just the US. The entire Ring of Fire, the fault line that virtually encircled the Pacific Ocean, had been disrupted. Hawaii, Fiji, and the Philippines were completely underwater, and the tsunamis that resulted had devastated what was left of Japan. It was just a matter of time before the Ramapo Fault near which their compound was situated, and that was previously heard from only as a whisper, became a source of widespread destruction as well.

The rain and hail that was driving against the mountain was unsettling, even though Russell knew his structure could withstand it. He had designed the framework himself, but the world had not been nearly so violent back then. Soon his previous expert designs would prove to be obsolete. Hopefully not this day. The powerful drumming on the panes had him on edge. He tried to reach Amira and her scouts to tell them to retreat and return to base, but she wasn't answering her radio. Probably interference from the storm. He frowned. No one should be outside in this.

He made his way down to the command center to find Jennifer, Angelo, Morgan O'Keefe, and Ricardo. Good, he thought. Both legs of security, a physicist, and IT.

"I can't reach Amira," Russell said. "I'm worried."

"She checked in ten minutes ago, just before the storm surge. She actually saw it coming. She should be on her way back, but that girl takes a lot of risks. I don't know… The rest of the search party just checked in," Ricardo said.

"What's our status?" Russell asked.

Jennifer spoke first. "The Q is secure within the ship. This polymantine is amazing. I don't think anything can break through it. Even if—God forbid—the mountain collapsed and destroyed the *Phoenix*, I think our little quantum baby would survive."

"What is it made of?" Angelo asked.

"Near as I could get from Dr. Simmons, it's a thin diamond film deposited on an alloy made from nickel, chromium, molybdenum, and niobium," Morgan said. "The underlying metal was patented as *Inconel*®, back in the days when patents were respected. We used something similar, mixed with titanium, for the hull of the *Phoenix*, which is incredibly strong, can withstand intense heat, and does not corrode. But when she placed a diamond film over it, she increased its impenetrability by 200 percent," Morgan answered.

Ricardo shook his head. "You lost me, but I trust you." He turned to Russell. "I'm trying to track this storm. It's huge and it's almost like it originated out of nowhere. It doesn't have a clear heading, so I can't tell you when it will pass."

"What about the seismic activity?" Russell asked.

"That seems to be settling down. Under the worst of circumstances, that's usually short lived." Ricardo chuckled. "The walls won't be coming down around us—not *this* time, anyway!"

Russell nodded and relaxed a little. He was worried about Amira, but the woman seemed to have mad survival skills. He was sure she had found a way to shelter and wait out the storm. As long as they weren't all going to get drawn down into the Earth's crust, they should be okay. He went back to the *Phoenix* to find Teresa. As expected, she was there with Steve Seltzer and Devon. They were in a heated debate.

"What's up?" Russell asked.

They all stopped suddenly. Steve and Teresa looked like a couple of puppies who'd been unraveling the toilet paper roll and just got caught. No one spoke, and Russell looked to each of them in turn. No one looked back. A minute passed, and then another.

"We don't know how to stop," Devon finally said.

"What are you talking about?"

Devon shrugged his shoulders. "The soliton. We can

generate it, we can aim the ship precisely to wherever we want to go, we can probably generate the energy to shoot us into space at several times the speed of light, and then we don't need to keep feeding it energy. Especially in outer space, if we plot our course correctly and avoid strong gravitational fields, there's essentially no resistance, so we can just...keep...going."

"This is a problem?" Russell asked. He was feeling impatient. There was so much going on, he wasn't in the mood for riddles.

No one answered, and slowly, it dawned on him. "Oh, I see."

Teresa looked sheepish and wouldn't meet his eyes. "I told you I found a way to travel at faster-than-light speed, with minimal energy requirements. And I did..."

Steve was shaking his head. "It's brilliant, really. I mean, absolutely brilliant. But here's the rub: Think of a soliton wave like a tsunami. Once it's been generated by the extreme energy of an earthquake or, say, an asteroid hitting the planet, it just travels. It has an extremely large wavelength, so we can see this mountain of water moving across the entire ocean. But the water itself doesn't really move much horizontally, it just goes up and down. It's the *energy wave* that propagates; the water is simply the medium it employs. It requires no further accelerant. But..." He took a deep breath. "The wave only stops when it runs out of its medium. *It stops when it hits the continent.*"

Russell's eyes opened wide. "We may have no choice but to leave in a day or two. I'm counting on you guys to—"

"Yeah, we know," Steve said.

"We're working out a way to use the sun's gravitational

field to whip us around and absorb the energy so we can slow down. It will be tricky, since we won't have exact data about the strength of the star until we are much nearer and then we will have to make calculations instantaneously," Teresa said. "We were considering whether we should make it a two-step process, like 'pumping the brakes,' so we can avoid getting so close to a sun and still be sure not to over-shoot, but that will prolong our travel time by a lot. Either way, we'll have to get close enough for the star to start pulling us in, but not so close that we can't break from its gravitational field. It's going to be a delicate move. We will be aiming for a star, not a planet."

"And if it doesn't work?" Russell asked.

Devon shrugged. "If it doesn't work, we just get sucked into the star and burn up," he said.

CHAPTER 25

Amira was dodging through the sheaves of corn as the first drops of rain began to fall. The temperature plummeted precipitously, and the rain quickly turned to hail. The wind whipped it around so fast, she couldn't effectively cover her face to protect herself from it. The corn was flying everywhere and even the hail was moving sideways. She nearly lost her firearm to the wind and had to fight to pull it back to her side. She kept going in the general direction she had seen Keter flee. Surely he couldn't be making much progress in this either. But the visibility decreased to little more than a few feet in front of her, and she realized she would never find anyone in this mess. And at certain point, she felt like she might even be thrown across the valley from the wind.

Amira was a slight but muscular woman. Weighing in at 138 pounds only because of her solid muscle mass, she was five feet four and wore a size two in most things. She crawled on her belly to the side of the valley and tried to shelter behind an apple tree, hoping it would not come down, but she was having trouble not getting blown away herself. She fished in her pack for some rope, which took forever. She wasn't exactly sure what that had cost her, as other equipment she had stashed flew out of reach as she searched. With sustained effort, she managed to tether herself to the tree trunk so she wouldn't be tossed across the valley, but as she had to let go of the pack for a moment to do so, she lost that into the tempest as well. She squatted down and waited. A storm like this had to pass quickly. At least, the "old Earth" could not sustain this much force for more than a quarter of an hour. She was soaked and freezing, but she hung on, dreaming about a hot cup of chocolate and a warm, dry blanket.

From the corner of her eye, she thought she saw movement—human movement. Peering through the whirlwind, she could have sworn there was a man walking between the apple trees, barely touched by the wind. Geez, she thought, I'm losing my mind. Seeing mirages, of all things. Just then, her tree was struck by a wind gust so strong, the trunk lifted up from the ground and twisted as it fell, exposing the large web of roots and pinning Amira to the ground. One of her legs was trapped under the tree. She sighted her pack on the ground, several feet away and totally unreachable. She looked for her knife in her belt to cut herself loose, but it was nowhere to be found. The knot she had tied was now on the other side of the tree trunk.

She struggled with the rope and then tried to at least push

the tree off her leg, but without success. It started to occur to her that this might not end well for her. Her radio, if she even knew where it had gone, would be nonfunctional from the storm interference, and even if she could call for help, how would anyone find her in this mess?

She was losing sensation in her leg, and she tried to tell herself it was just from the cold, that she was going to be fine as soon as the storm lessened, and she could get inside. Maybe she had an abrasion or even a break, but she would heal. As she told herself this, she glanced down and saw the puddles forming around her shin were turning pink. And then red. She needed to get free, to tamponade whatever was bleeding. She struggled harder to extricate her leg and then started to feel the pain. Was that a good sign or a bad one? Amira, who had never cried out for anyone in her adult life, screamed for help as loud as she could, but her voice was lost in the roar of the wind.

Eventually, Amira passed out. No longer aware of anything, not even the storm, she seemed to float in some other world. She found herself looking down on her soaked, inert body, lying in a pool of blood.

The sky had grown so dark, it could have been midnight, but as she looked up to pray, there was a small bright spot above her, which eerily intensified until she was sure she was looking directly at the sun. The sun, shrouded in the blackness of night; the sky was both light and dark at the same time, with the violent wind deafening and ever present. She was hallucinating. This is the end, she thought. She whispered the *shemah* in her head, a last prayer to God, and closed her eyes, feeling the torrents of the cyclone protesting her fixed position, as if it were angered that it could not pluck her free and fling her away. But the vision of the sun at midnight remained.

She did not know how long she lay there, but the wind seemed to subside, and a peaceful silence enveloped her. The roaring of the wind seemed to belong to some other place as Amira accepted her death. Dimly, she felt the movement of the apple tree, the freeing of her leg, and she was sure that God was calling her home to Him; she prepared to rise into the storm and into the otherworld.

Her eyes opened slightly. There was a man kneeling at her side, about the only visible thing she could focus on through the swirling corn and rain. Everything else was a blur in the gale-force wind. He had disentangled the rope from the tree and released her leg from under the fallen trunk. With a strip of cloth, acquired from where, Amira did not know, he tightened a torniquet around her leg until the bleeding stopped and positioned her in the hollow of the tree where the wind was diminished. Then he took her own radio and put it on the emergency setting, so that it would transmit her location with a continuous SOS signal and placed it in her hand, closing her fingers tightly around it. Why hadn't she thought of that? Oh, right, the storm had taken her radio; she had lost it somewhere far away from here. Surely this must all be a dream.

The man produced a waterproof blanket and wrapped her shoulders in it, tenting it to cover her head, and the sound of the wind seeped back into her brain, less ferocious now. Amira realized she was shivering uncontrollably and decided she must be alive, if only because she imagined dead people didn't shiver.

The man leaned in close to speak over the wind, and she could see his face for the first time. "They will come for you. Hang on," he said. And then he was gone, leaving Amira alone and astonished. The man was Sahina Keter.

CHAPTER 26

Justine Ganaffe had brought her small board together in the Cabinet Room for an update. It was reported that two scouts had been sent out to the area of the suspected resistance stronghold several weeks ago, but no one had heard from them at all in the last week. After the coordinates of Arnold Higgins's little explosion that ended his life were verified, a small squad of fighter planes was sent to evaluate and eliminate the rebel's position.

There had been some duplicity around the coordinates received, as the transmitter seemed to come from two different places in succession and shouldn't have been activated until the goal was reached. And then the ghastly storm arose out of nowhere and the instrument guidance systems failed. Contact was lost with each of the planes, which may have crashed, for all they knew. Justine demanded to know where their operatives on the ground were, but no one had heard from either of them.

"Okay," Justine said to her menagerie. "Let's assume the operatives are dead and all four planes went down. Where is the last place they were headed to? That's where we have to focus on as soon as the storm breaks. And we need to find those scientists who escaped. The lab was stripped, and they apparently removed several pieces of the research that are essential for us to successfully move on to our next destination. I'm going to need volunteers to continue the search, people I can trust."

No one raised their hand. Generally speaking, volunteering for anything in the Ganaffe circle meant sacrificing your own life. Everyone was expendable. Justine turned to Jansen.

"Jansen."

"Ma'am," he answered.

"You have a young child, don't you? You want him to grow up in a secure place, on a planet that is at peace and that provides abundantly, do you not?"

"Yes, ma'am."

"I want you to go out and find our operatives. And find this refuge. Sentics will accompany you."

John Sentics was sipping his coffee, and it went sputtering over his papers in front of him. All eyes turned to him. His face was bright red.

"You have a problem with that?" Justine asked.

John was silent. The last six years had given him a false sense of security. He had risen to senior adviser, and it fell on him to train the newbies. Although he always told his charges that no one's life was a given, he had forgotten that he was not and had never been part of the Ganaffe Inner Circle. His life was not guaranteed either. He didn't have family waiting for him—not that he could have expected to ever see them again if he did. But he did value taking breath each day. He glanced at Jansen and gauged their chances of survival together on the outside.

Jansen had a handsome face, but he was soft, like a man who had never held a barbell a day in his life, and he was not particularly smart either. John assumed Justine kept him around for his slightly sensual, cavalier attitude and his willingness to role-play with her in whatever way she chose. He seemed too dumb to do otherwise, in John's opinion. Of late, Justine had apparently asked some unusual things of Jansen in the bedroom that involved her shackling him in chains and wrapping leather somewhat tightly around his neck, and he must have complied, though likely not willingly; the scars were quite visible. His haughty attitude may have just cost him his life. Justine was a cold and cruel woman, outperformed in that arena only by her father. Some postulated that President Martine Ganaffe had personally trained his daughter in his techniques, possibly also in the bedroom.

John's mind was moving a mile a minute. It was probably safe to assume that he was never coming back here. No one who had ever failed on a mission had returned to their former status, and no one who had succeeded lived to tell about it. No one that he knew of, anyway. If he was going to survive, he decided, he would have to ditch Jansen and find a way to escape. But to where? He had a sister he had not spoken to in years, but if he went there, they'd find him. He tried not to think about what would happen to his sister if he did *not* go there, since it was the first place Justine would look.

At forty years old, John had been a loyal servant to President Ganaffe and then to Justine when Ganaffe himself ceased to make appearances several years ago. Things were different now, yes, but he thought *his* situation was secure. All that was about to change, and John hated change.

"Tell me your wishes and I shall carry them out," John said to Justine, feeling like an imposter. But he really had no choice. He repeated it to himself: he really had no choice.

CHAPTER 27

The storm had finally dissipated enough for Angelo to pick up the radio SOS. A crew of five men and women went out to find the source. While Angelo had suspected it was Amira—it was her radio transmitting—with the recent threats, it could have also been a trap. The crew set out fully armed as well as with first aid and transport equipment. They found her half-conscious in the hollow of a fallen apple tree, gripping the radio so hard that at first, the medic thought she was in rigor mortis. The surrounding corn crop was in shambles, and getting an unconscious, near dead-weight woman over the torn up fields was quite a challenge. They got her inside and to their hospital wing, where Dr. Lister did a careful exam and concluded that while Amira suffered from mild hypothermia, the only significant traumatic injury was a broken fibula. However, there had been substantial blood loss from the lacerated anterior tibial artery as it wrapped laterally around the lower aspect of the shin. A few small parts of the tree trunk were still embedded in Amira's leg, and one still pressing against the artery itself was probably all that had kept her from bleeding out completely—that and the quizzically lifesaving tourniquet that she had apparently managed to tie off.

When Braelyn got down to the recovery room, Amira was barely awake. She was wrapped in heated blankets and receiving blood and IV fluids, and she was as weak as a kitten. Braelyn couldn't shake the feeling of guilt that she hadn't known Amira was in trouble. She should never have been left out there alone like that.

Russell was suddenly at her side. "It was her choice, Brae. And once the skies opened up like that, we could not have reached her. The cyclone happened so fast, and with such furor, it just wasn't possible."

"Yeah? Well, we have to do better, especially when we go off-world. We can't leave our people to fend for themselves. No matter who they are. We *have* to take care of each other, Russell! This was inexcusable."

Russell looked at her sideways.

"I know," Braelyn said, "you're thinking I don't even like Amira much. That doesn't matter. And that was…before, anyway. She's incredibly valuable to our team, and—and— she's one of us. Tell me this will *never* happen again!"

"What will never happen? Brae, we are going into perilous conditions. We will be landing—hopefully—on a planet where we can breathe the air, but we won't know the terrain, we won't know what is edible and what is poison to us, we won't know the weather conditions, or even if there will be raw materials to build shelters. Hell, Brae, if it will support us, there's a mighty good chance there will already be intelligent life living there. They may welcome us or attack us. Or perhaps they will just ignore us, but what if we unknowingly step all over their sacred things or eat what they consider sacrosanct, or just interfere too much with their ecosystem? We *belonged* on planet Earth. We will not *belong* anywhere else. Not at first, anyway. Get used to it."

Braelyn bit her lip. She had rarely seen Russell get this emotional. She *reached* for him tentatively and felt his fear. Raw terror, hovering at the limits of his consciousness. But she also realized her reaction to Amira's near death had incited the same sort of fear in herself.

"We will have to prepare everyone. Make it clear how dangerous it will be," she said in a whisper.

Amira stirred and groaned softly. The quiet beeping of her monitor increased its rate, and Tobi came in to check on her patient.

Amira awoke abruptly then and tried to sit up. She seemed to be almost in a panic as she grabbed the handrails and pulled on them.

"Whoa there," Tobi Lister said softly. "Take it easy, you're okay."

At that moment, Russell's radio went off, and he stepped out to answer Angelo in private, leaving the two women with Amira.

Braelyn lifted the back of the gurney so Amira could sit up. "You're lucky to be alive. Why didn't you come right back when the storm started?"

Amira squeezed her eyes shut tightly as if she was trying to remember—or maybe—trying to forget. "So fast...it just came up so fast," Amira said softly. "I tried... I couldn't find shelter. The wind was going in circles. Was there a tornado?"

"There were squalls in the valley," Braelyn said. "You might have been in one of them."

"I thought it was going to pick me up and throw me, like *The Wizard of Oz*." She gave them a half smile. "I don't know how I'm alive. I thought I had died."

Tobi was checking her IV rate. "You almost did. If you hadn't gotten that tourniquet on… How did you manage that in the storm?"

"I don't—I didn't!"

"What do you mean, 'you didn't'?" Braelyn said. "It didn't appear all by itself and tie off exactly at the spot where you were bleeding from."

Amira grabbed Braelyn's wrist. "It was him."

"Who?" Braelyn asked.

Russell came back in and interrupted tersely. "You okay?" he asked Amira. "I'm going up to the command center. That device Keter was using… he wasn't guiding the planes in. Looks like he was deflecting them away. I don't know what he is about, but we need to find him. He can't be conducting operations, for or against us, without telling us what he's doing."

"He saved my life," Amira said quietly.

They all looked at her.

"He cut me out of the rope when the tree fell. He put on the torniquet. He left me with the radio. I don't know why. It doesn't make sense."

"We are going to have to reevaluate this Sahina Keter," Braelyn said.

"Yeah? First we have to find him," Russell said as he headed for the door.

CHAPTER 28

ussell assembled the community in their large meeting hall. When they had first built the complex, there had only been a couple of hundred of them, and he had been shocked to have so many. He felt like the place would never sustain them. But over the years, more and more desperate people began finding their way in. Some of them highly skilled, some of them just terrified and willing to work—doing anything—to be in a safe place. They often came as families with young children, and since they had a couple of teachers and a vast array of digital knowledge and teaching materials available, they set up a school. The hope was that one day, life would return to something akin to normal and they would be able to reintegrate back into a civilized society. Somewhere along the way, that dream started to fade.

In the beginning, Russell did his best to accommodate anyone who asked for admittance, as long as they were good people and were not just looking for a handout but who were willing to help in any way they could. As their needs grew, they built further into the mountainside. Gradually, the stream of newcomers had slowed to a trickle as the GGP made travel without a permit impossible, and obtaining a permit meant knowing exactly where you wanted to go; the compound did not exactly have a searchable address. How they grew to a community of twenty-five hundred was mind boggling, but before Teresa and Devon had been rescued, they had been stagnant in numbers for over a year. Except, of course, for the new baby, born six months ago.

The man named Harris had extracted a promise from Russell when they established themselves. Harris provided a defense system such as Russell had never imagined—and had never envisioned they would need. He required only that Russell, with his peculiar sight into people's minds, evaluate each person entering and assure that they were not controlled by the GGP under the influence of scopolamine, and that he make sure they were people of 'good heart'—whatever that meant. Russell was conscientious about it for the first several years, but he admittedly had slacked off as the number of people seeking sanctuary declined. Now he wondered: Were there people with ill intentions among them? There was no time now to interview everyone who wanted to come with them to the stars.

Russell stood by the podium feeling anxious. He didn't usually get nervous; he just did whatever the situation at hand required, but a part of him was dreading this forum. Braelyn was onstage with him, as were their physicists, Morgan O'Keefe and Steve Seltzer. He had asked Teresa to join them as well, and she had complied reluctantly. She was still fearful about being seen in public, even knowing that the chances of anyone from the GGP being in the audience were next to zero.

Jennifer, their genius computer expert, was also there but off to the side. Angelo and Ricardo were on the sidelines with their radios, keeping in touch with those monitoring the security station and the climate alerts. Troy DeJacob had offered to stay up top and watch for early signs of any severe weather activity.

A few minutes after 7:00 p.m., it appeared that everyone who planned to join had arrived, and the discussion was being broadcasted to anyone's rooms who could not or did not wish to come into the great hall. Russell raised his hands ever so slightly, and the room became eerily silent. Russell licked his lips.

"Thank you all for coming. This is a difficult conversation to have. I think we've been fairly comfortable here for the last decade, safe from the GGP and sheltered, for the most part, from the extreme weather. It feels like we've set down roots. Our families are growing, and we have established a life apart.

"But there have been some recent, disturbing changes. And change is always a challenge.

"As many of you have realized, the weather patterns have become more and more dangerous and unpredictable. We have less time to batten down for storms, and the storms are more violent. Yesterday's tempest took most of our cornfields."

There was some murmuring in the room.

"In addition to that," Russell continued, "we have been discovered." The murmuring grew louder. "As of this moment, we seem to have evaded attack, and as many of you know, we do have defenses. Using those defenses, however, would attract even more unwanted attention, and resisting the military power of the United States… well, I'm not sure that's possible. The best we can hope for is to stall while we escape. I don't think winning is an option."

There, he had said it. And now the room erupted in agitated chatter and there was fear in many residents' eyes. Russell looked over at Braelyn, who came to stand beside him. In a rare show of affection and solidarity, she reached for his hand behind the podium. Russell felt immeasurable gratitude. He was acutely aware of how dispassionate he came across, and in truth, he kept most of his own feelings stuffed comfortably away, but he was always subject to the onslaught of the emotions of others. Right now, he desperately wanted to console these people, but what he had to offer might not be at all what they were looking for.

Reluctantly, Russell released Braelyn and raised his hands again. When he got to shoulder level, the room quieted expectantly.

"We have anticipated both of these matters, and we," he looked around at his staff behind him on the stage, "we have been looking for solutions for several years now." A pregnant silence greeted this news. Finally, Russell blurted it out. "We have been looking for ways to move off-world."

He expected a loud reaction, but the group seemed stunned. Someone coughed, but you could have heard a needle drop at the back of the room. It was that quiet.

Russell looked behind him to his physicists. He noticed that Angie and Arthur Engman had joined them; they were the mechanical engineers who had designed the initial version of the *Phoenix,* and they were overseeing the modifications recommended by Teresa.

Russell glanced at Angelo, who nodded back. They had prearranged that the *Phoenix* needed to be well guarded in the event some malcontent, not willing to take their chances off-world, might try to sabotage everyone else, so as not to be left behind alone. Angelo's nod was verification that the ship was protected. Up until now, the majority of their population had no idea what the "project" going on underground was about.

Angie stepped up to the podium and touched Russell gently on the elbow, and gratefully, he and Braelyn stepped back a few paces. Angie was one of those ultra-perceptive people, and she seemed to see right through Russell's impassivity and sense the torrents of sentiment below. Russell thought if she hadn't been married to Arthur, she might have pursued a more intimate relationship, but he found her unnerving, and was glad he could sidestep the issue. Except that right now, he thoroughly appreciated her taking the focus off him for a few moments.

Angie cleared her throat. "Some of you may have wondered what the construction in the mountain on the west side of the complex is about. We have built a ship. A ship that can carry us to another planet for colonization." She looked around, but still, no one said a word. She took a deep breath. "We are confident that the ship will withstand the lengthy flight to another solar system."

"That will take forever!" said a voice in the crowd. "We will all die of old age on such a journey!" Everyone started talking at once then, and there was anger, fear, and a few affirmations of gratitude audible in the crowd. Angie was unable to restore order.

Russell stepped back up. He tapped his mike so it made a loud, grating sound and waited for the crowd to settle down. "Please hold your questions. We know you have many, many questions. We are going to explain everything. Give us a chance and we will be happy to address remaining queries when we're finished."

They took turns then, Steve, Teresa, Jennifer. Explaining in fundamental language that the ship would be traveling at faster-than-light speed, that they had a quantum computer to calculate trajectories, and that they had selected several potential planets that could be expected to support human life. They didn't get much further than that.

"What if we don't want to go?" a faceless voice asked.

Russell came back to the front of the stage to speak. His voice was solemn. "Staying is a valid and reasonable choice, and I would like each of you to carefully consider all the factors." He licked his lips and took a moment to continue.

"Make no mistake. If you choose to embark on this journey, there will be many challenges. And there is a risk that we may not make it safely to our destination. We may die in space."

He took a moment to look around at the reactions of the group. "Assuming we land intact, and assuming we land on a habitable planet, we will have to find raw materials with which to build shelters. We will have to find food sources. We will have to navigate whatever the local weather is, and we will have to find materials to make the products most of us take for granted. Even toilet paper will be different." Russell smiled, and a few people snickered.

"In addition, and perhaps as important, there may well already be sentient life on this other planet. We will have to be sensitive to their needs and desires. Think of how humans would have felt if a colony of aliens touched down, say, in the Great Plains, and wanted to settle.

"We will be the intruders. We must establish ourselves as a cooperative, compassionate race, willing to take our cue from the resident sapient life form. To be helpful if we can. To guard against insulting them even in ways we do not understand. We must embody the opposite values of what the United States has been living by for the last decade."

"What if they tell us to get the hell out?" another voice shouted. "What if they attack us?"

"That is also a real possibility," Russell answered. "We will be bringing weapons with us, but they are for self-defense only. It is going to be imperative that we be certain that another species' actions are intended as hostile before we engage them in anything but deflecting what could be harmful to us.

"This journey is not for the faint of heart." Russell looked directly at the man who had asked the question. He recognized him as Gregory Davidica, who had shown up with his family about three years ago. He'd had his wife and two of his children with him, then six and eight; his two-year-old had been tortured and killed by the Whispies. Russell had been concerned that he'd be too rageful to live peacefully among them, but he had safely and responsibly discharged his anger in karate lessons, where he had excelled in a persistent and controlled manner.

He was now about thirty-one; he had just finished vet school when he had arrived but had never gotten a chance to practice. There was not much work for a veterinarian here in the compound, but he had assisted Dr. Lister in the medical unit. He and his family had found peace and safety here, but now he was being asked if he wanted to take his wife and remaining children to a completely different world and risk their lives in a whole different way.

"Gregory," Russell said, "if you decide to join us, your training will be invaluable, as we do not know what kind of animal life we will encounter." Russell addressed the group again.

"All of you have skills that we will need in the colonization of a new planet. But let me be clear: No one is required to leave. We *anticipated* that some will want to stay. Anyone who wishes to stay behind will be able to remain here, and the compound will be left to you completely intact, including the operational defense systems, and we will provide reference guides on equipment and the running of the complex." He licked his lips again. Here was the hardest part. "In truth, the ship will only fit about fifteen hundred, which is about sixty percent of us. If more than that wish to come into space, we will have to draw lots."

The room erupted again. Everyone was shouting and talking at once, and Teresa came to Russell's side. "How will we keep this from becoming a riot?" she asked.

Russell shook his head. "I don't believe they will become destructive. They are afraid, understandably, but destruction of this hold is a suicide venture. I have faith in them. I met each of them—or most, at least—as they arrived. They are all good people or they would not be here at all."

Another clear voice rang out as a woman stood up on a table to be heard. "When is this happening?"

CHAPTER 29

ohn and Jansen were outfitted in camouflage fatigues to blend in with the forest floor and given radios and weapons. John glanced sideways at Jansen, trying to size him up. Would he be any good in a fight? Did he understand that they were as good as dead now to the GGP? Could he be enlisted as an ally or would he follow the party line literally to the bitter end?

There were no experimental intelligence guards accompanying them, which John supposed was designed to give him an illusion of security, since John had designed the protocols for sending the Unthinking along on suicide missions. But that didn't mean they weren't being tracked. Was it in his equipment, his pack—his clothes? He could not hope to make an escape until he found the transmitters and rid himself of them. For all he knew, he was bugged as well, and they would hear if he spoke to Jansen about their future. John knew all their tricks, and worse, they knew he knew their tricks, so perhaps they had gotten creative. He certainly would have.

They traveled by motorcycle, much like the Marauders did, with their hair slicked back and knives in their belts in addition to semiautomatics slung over their shoulders, and people gave them a wide berth. The difference was, they weren't drunk, firing into the air and into crowds, or hooting and howling as they went along. A real Marauder would know the difference, but others did not want to know.

John looked around in curiosity. He had not been out of the White House in six years. The streets in DC were dirty and the shops were trashed, with shattered glass lining the sidewalks. A few beggars disappeared into the shadows when they heard the bikes coming down the road. There were a few broken down cars along the sides of the avenues, but nothing that appeared drivable. Probably anything with wheels that could carry anyone had been stolen. Old Alexandria looked like it had been thrown back into Civil War times.

Jansen seemed unfazed by their surroundings. He was in his late twenties and had only joined the White House staff eighteen months ago. The word was, he had been about to be executed at the time. He pleaded for his life and praised President Ganaffe so ardently that they brought him in; he petitioned Justine to let him live, saying he would be forever useful to her. She certainly had used him enough in her private suite. Amazing that her husband, Murray, either didn't know or didn't care what she did. Unless she had so damaged her husband as to make Murray a eunuch. John chuckled at that thought. It would serve Murray right for being such a pansy ass.

As they got out of the city and onto Route 95, it was like

leaving civilization behind altogether. It could have been another planet entirely. The damage along the highway from the storms was extensive, and not a soul was in sight. Not on foot and not in a vehicle of any sort. It looked like something out of a Stephen King book.

Driving through Baltimore was much the same as DC, and there was certainly no traffic even at 9:30 a.m. At 95 mph, they were through it in fifteen minutes and headed north to Philly and then beyond into Staten Island, where they'd been told they could still fill the tanks. Most of the gas stations were dry or nonfunctional. For a split second, John wondered about the sanity of driving through Manhattan as two lone bikers. Jansen dismissed John's suggestion to go north through New Jersey; he seemed to thrive on seeing dead bodies and burned-out buildings, and he whooped his way obnoxiously through the length of Manhattan Island. The streets were uncannily deserted.

Nevertheless, there was a feeling of being watched from alleyways and behind broken down cars; certainly no one could have missed their presence. New York City had always been a hard place to break. New Yorkers were tough and had an attitude that they could withstand anything. For a city that was once divided by gangs and violence, the remaining rebels who huddled here had proven surprisingly hard to persuade to join the GGP. But then they had always had a deleteriously liberal attitude, long before Ganaffe had come to power. Even though Ganaffe himself was born and raised here and had made most of his fortune on these very streets, his own city had rejected him.

There was absolutely no food to be found—not that John would have trusted to consume it anyway. But what were these people eating? And there were most definitely people still living here. Fortunately, he and Jansen had brought their own food supplies.

Once they passed through Westchester, there was no clear route. Before the scientists' escape, a message to Dr. Richard Simmons had been intercepted indicating there was an encampment somewhere in the northern Appalachians. But the mountain range was huge; did they know for sure they should be looking in the Catskills? Why not the Adirondacks?

John had been consulting his map and the extent of the mountain range was massive. What if they should have been going south to the Smokey's? Did they *really* know this place was in the northeast mountains? The Appalachians spanned almost the entire east side of the country for two thousand miles, from Alabama to Canada, and the Appalachian Trail itself, winding in places, was nearly twenty-three hundred miles long. There were hundreds of secondary trails and caves to hole up in and create little invisible communities—if they hadn't been destroyed by storms, that was. A person could survive a long time if they were close to a spring and could trap their own food. A person could… but could a community?

They continued roughly north until Jansen pulled off the side of the road to relieve himself, and found a discarded bike in a ditch, as if someone had tried to hide it there. But on second glance, it looked mangled and probably no longer roadworthy. John scouted around and found a jacket much like the ones he and Jansen had been outfitted in, which made him suspicious. They continued walking off the road and into the tree line, while constantly checking over their shoulders.

John nearly tripped over something fleshy and on closer look, thought he would start retching.

At his feet was a corpse, partially decomposed, with dried blood all over leaves that had turned red and gold anyway with the season. John was not a stranger to death, but the difference was the GGP-issued pistol in the figure's belt. Gingerly, he picked it up and examined it. The clip was empty; the mystery of at least one of their operatives was solved.

Jansen looked grim as he stood over the dead man for several minutes.

"I knew him," Jansen said. "His name was Tony. We were buds."

John stepped aside and took out his radio to report the finding and ask for additional orders. He got what he expected, to keep moving forward and look for the second operative. And if they found the encampment, they should transmit those coordinates immediately and then attempt to gain access.

John signed off and looked at Jansen, who was still staring at the corpse. "Do you... do you want to bury him?" John asked.

Jansen shrugged. "Nah. Ain't nothing to bury him with. We ain't got no shovels. Besides, we'd best be on our way." He turned and started heading back to their motorcycles.

"Yeah, but which way?" John asked, looking to the tall trees in front of him for advice.

CHAPTER 30

Russell looked at the agitated crowd. "We need to leave as soon as possible. It will be in the next few days. You will each be getting a survey on your tablets in the next hour, and I'd like you all to think about it and submit your response by noon tomorrow. There's a lot to do to prepare, both for those coming and for those staying."

There was a lot of muttering and restlessness, but people shuffled out of the great hall. It was 8:30 p.m., and Russell doubted anyone was going to be getting much sleep that night.

The leadership team gathered on the stage.

"Well, cat's out of the bag," Jennifer said. "I think they took it rather well, all things considered."

Steve Seltzer was shaking his head. "There were very few questions. I'd have thought they'd want more explanation, and—and understanding of how this will work."

Morgan looked up. "That's because you're a physicist.

You have a *need* to know how the universe works. Most people just want to go along for the ride. They want someone to tell them everything is going to be okay so they don't have to put any effort into it themselves."

"But this is their future—their lives!" Steve shouted. "Don't they want to evaluate the dangers; don't they want to know more about what they might be up against? Do these people even understand that if we go to another planet, *everything* will be different? Geez, *I* have a million questions!"

Braelyn chimed in. "Some do. I got the sense that most feel like if we are going, we have already worked out the risks. They've trusted us all these years, why should that change? Oh, seriously, Steve, do you really think most people put that much energy into thinking about their lives? Come on!"

"If they have children, especially, they should," Jennifer said quietly. "But maybe they just understand that we can't remain here. Or maybe the questions will come later, maybe they're just shell shocked right now."

"Are all of you here committed to going?" Angelo surprised them with the question, but it needed to be asked.

"Yes, I am," Morgan said, "but I'm not sure I'm *comfortable* with it. I mean, it was one thing to think about this in the theoretical sense, quite another to be actually planning to do it. You know, when I was a kid, I thought, 'Wouldn't it be cool to be an astronaut?' but that was to go on an adventure. I never considered leaving our planet *forever*. I wish… I wish I'd been able to find my brother. I wish he could come. Or at least, I wish I could tell him I'm going." Morgan's eyes were tearful, and they were all quiet. Every one of them had lost someone dear in the last few years. Whether to certain death or to the unknown.

"Everyone get some rest," Russell said. "Let's meet back in the conference room at 0600 hours. Think about this long and hard for yourselves. No one is required to come. But I'd be lying if I said our crew was not in dire need of every one of you."

They dispersed slowly and Teresa fell into step alongside Russell. "Where's Devon?" Russell asked.

"He felt self-conscious about being up here as part of the 'leadership,' given his age and his newness to the community. He was listening at the periphery. He will come. His father sacrificed his life to make this trip possible. He will not dishonor that."

"You make it sound like he wishes he could stay here somehow."

"Don't we all?" Teresa asked. "Don't we all wish we had not abdicated our freedom to those monsters? Don't we wish we had cared better for our dear Mother Earth?" Teresa brushed at her eye. "But most people will not take steps to change their life or their circumstance until death literally stares them in the face. So here we are. And as Morgan said, many *still* are looking for someone else to make the tough decisions."

"Who was it who said most people tiptoe their way through life hoping to make it safely to death?" Russell asked.

Teresa chuckled. "Some very observant soul, to be sure. See you in the morning."

Instead of going straight to her room, she looked for Devon and found him in one of the common rooms with

Amira. Amira was wearing a sturdy, long ortho boot on her left leg, and there were crutches propped up next to her. Her left leg was up on a table, and she and Devon were sitting side by side on a couch. Teresa joined them and sat in a chair opposite. None of them spoke for several minutes. Teresa wondered what intimate conversation she had just interrupted, but she hadn't spent any time with her son in days, and there was too much turmoil all around them for her to leave them to themselves as she might have done if times were normal.

"Dad should be here," Devon finally said. "He worked so hard for this."

Teresa nodded. "He would be so pleased that we made it, that all our work was being applied for the rescue of good people. Not those…scum."

Teresa surprised herself with the word, but she was so disgusted with the GGP, the Whispies with their little soldier Marauders, and a population that either believed in White Supremacy or just went along the easy way and couldn't be bothered speaking up. She felt a prickling on her neck, like she was being watched, and looked up to see Amira staring at her intently. "What?" Teresa asked.

Amira looked startled and turned away. "Sorry," she said. "I didn't mean to stare. You have risked so much, and now here you are, ready to risk much more. I am assuming you believe it will all work. The ship, your calculations, the warp… You wouldn't get on that ship if you didn't believe we had a better than even chance, right?"

Teresa passed her hands through her dark, coarse hair. It was shorter than Amira's, who wore her hair below the shoulder, but both women had tight curls of different textures that gave their heads a bushy look, and both women had different shades of olive skin.

"I do believe it," Teresa said. "We've been over and over everything for a year. We were so excited, but afraid to share it with anyone. We knew if the GGP found out, they would suck it out of us and then kill us to keep it secret. They found out anyway. They plan to leave the world to be run by the Whispies and their drunken plebes, who are addicted to cruelty. They will also head to the stars, and they are bringing slaves with them."

Teresa felt like she might vomit and couldn't go on. She looked at Devon and he nodded. "The planet is beyond salvation," he said quietly. "My dad and I analyzed everything. There's maybe another three or four years before it's bound to have some sort of extinction event. Only pockets of people can hope to survive after that, and probably not for long; the ecosystems have already changed so dramatically."

Amira looked wide-eyed. "Do Russell and Braelyn know this? Shouldn't this be presented to the entire community for them to weigh in making their decision?"

Devon shrugged but Teresa answered. "These are all probabilities. We are also dealing in probabilities when we say we can make it safely to another solar system and find a planet that is both habitable and accepting of us. It's all an enormous gamble."

"I guess..." Amira said. She nodded at her leg and clenched her fists. "I know I should be grateful—I could easily have died chasing that guy. But what an awful time to break a leg. I feel so useless. Devon said we plan to leave in a few days; I wonder if being in space will affect the way the bone heals."

"That probably depends on how much we use gravity on board ship. It's the stress on the bones that stimulates growth," Teresa answered.

"But here on Earth, Tobi told me not to put weight on it anyway, so what's the difference in space? She also said the radiation could be a factor… Apparently human physiology in space has different parameters. I know Tobi has read a ton on it. She's amazing. Do you know she has a collection of microbes that can actually be genetically directed to produce a variety of antibiotics? It never occurred to me that medicine has a shelf life and will expire. Or that we might need different pharmaceuticals in space." Amira shook her head in wonder.

"Try not to worry, Amira," Teresa said. "We are in unmapped territory, but we will learn as we go. As for your leg, even when it is elevated here at home, as you are wise to do, gravity is still operating all around you. It affects our physiology on every level, not just the rate at which bone is broken down and new bone is formed, but even how our blood travels throughout our bodies, clots, or responds to infection. I know researchers were doing studies of space medicine before everything broke down, but most of what medicine knows is currently understood in terms of the normal planetary forces that act on us. Gravity does not only affect what is rooted on the ground but also what is suspended in the air."

"Right," Amira said. "We also have no idea what health effects moving at faster-than-light speed will have on our bodies. I'm glad Tobi is coming with us, even if she is a bit older. I hope the journey won't be too hard on her. Now I'm afraid my leg may not heal at all." She reached down and started massaging it.

Teresa shook her head. "I didn't say that. And what do I know, anyway? I'm not a physician. I'm just saying these are uncharted grounds."

Amira looked pale. "I can't stay here when you go... I can't stay...and Tobi said this isn't a major injury. She said I'll make a full recovery. Surely she took into account that I would be in space."

Teresa wasn't sure Dr. Lister had any idea when they were scheduled to leave, nor was she sure the good doctor had accounted for all the unknown forces that would be acting on her patient. But she said none of this. "Dr. Lister is a great doctor. I would go with her advice."

CHAPTER 31

John and Jansen continued on their motorcycles, heading roughly north up Route 87. What used to be called the Tappanzee Bridge did not look stable enough to drive on. Some of the suspension posts were damaged, no doubt from one of any of the last violent storms, and it was swaying even in the minimal wind, so they decided to stay on the east side of the Hudson River, at least until it narrowed further on. But finally John signaled Jansen to stop.

Jansen looked reluctant. He was obviously having a great time cruising the open road.

"We're never going to find this place on the freeway," John said. "It's going to be tucked away somewhere. We've got to figure out where to look besides an asphalt highway."

"Yeah, but it's just so glorious being out here! Don't you feel it?" Jansen's remarks took John completely by surprise. Sure, it was gorgeous; it was 52 degrees with a slight wind, the skies were clear, and the trees were a myriad of colors—those trees that were still standing and had leaves, anyway. And they'd both been locked away for what seemed like forever, but John had thought Jansen was so loyal to the GGP as to be almost one of the Unthinking. He realized he really didn't know the younger man at all.

"They may be listening to us, you know," John said as softly as he could while still hoping to be heard.

"So what? Do you think they're coming for us? If they could do this themselves, they wouldn't send the likes of us. They just want to get rid of us and hope we can prove ourselves useful on our way to hell. You don't actually think they're going to take care of us out here, do ya?"

John was stunned. Not by the sentiment, but by the brazen statement. He had thought of Jansen as a pliable servant. Of course, he certainly had a valid point. They were dead men anyway, why not enjoy their last hours of life?

"I know..." John started. "I guess...maybe it's just habit by now."

"That's what they count on," Jansen said. "That witch-whore did her worst to me, made me her slave, tortured me, and beat me with chains and leather, all the while dosing me up with Viagra and anything else that would make me perform for her. I did it to survive. I sold myself, body and soul. But that's over now. I'm free and I ain't never going back. You can threaten me or shoot me, I'd rather die out here than in that prison." Jansen took a deep, exaggerated breath of the clean air. "One thing all these storms have done is clean the air. Taste it, man!

John was in shock. Sure, he wanted to make a run for it, find his family, get away. But he never dreamed Jansen would, and he wasn't quite sure where to start looking for the people he once loved. "So you want to abandon the mission?"

"Mission? What mission?" Jansen laughed. He stretched his arms out wide. "I'm just living in *this* moment. In *this* moment, we're free. Breathe it! Taste it! It might be gone in an hour. We might be dead. They might send a jet to shoot us down. But I don't care. I'll sacrifice everything for this *one* moment."

John said nothing, but on impulse, he stretched his arms out like Jansen was doing. It felt *so* good. He took a deep breath. Yes, he was alive, could feel alive, was more than the plebe who had followed the GGP in all things for so many years. Suddenly it hit him: he had not been eating recently. He just had no appetite of late, and even though he knew all the food except for the Ganaffes' was laced with scopolamine, it was less concentrated in the upstairs food that he normally ate, so Justine's minions would be more efficient. And it was wearing off.

"Hey, Jansen, did you stop eating the food?"

"That spiked shit? Yeah. Ages ago. I ate Justine's leftovers, right out of the garbage when she wasn't looking. I know, that's how she controls everyone, right?"

John nodded. So Jansen was really his own person now. John had completely misjudged him! "What do you want to do? Do you not want to find the rebel base?"

"Hell, I do! But I want to ask them to take me in. 'Course they might assume I'm a spy and kill me—that's what I'd do. But it would be worth the effort. Either that, or just head to the Appalachian Trail and live off the land until they either find me and kill me or I get killed by a bear or a local. You wanna turn me in, do it. I don't care. Like I said: I. Ain't. Never. Going. Back. Period."

With that, Jansen hopped back on his bike and sped off down the highway, whooping and howling as he went. John watched him until he was just a tiny speck on the distant road.

CHAPTER 32

Six a.m. came early, probably since most hadn't fallen asleep until somewhere around four in the morning. Russell noticed absently that Amira and Devon were sitting next to each other in the conference room, and Devon was securing her crutches behind them against the wall. Funny, he never pictured Amira as letting anyone do anything for her, as if it would somehow expose some weakness.

Everyone looked exhausted. Russell's nephew, Joshua, shuffled in; the first time Russell had seen him since the cyclone. He had been outside for a couple of days with a crew trying to clear away the destroyed crops left by the storm. Even though they were leaving—he assumed Joshua was coming—they didn't want a mess left in their wake for those staying behind.

Braelyn went and sat down next to her son, and they were speaking quietly. Suddenly the room was full. Ricardo and

Angelo each looked like they'd been up all night. Teresa sat straight and composed, as always. Russell wondered if anything ever rattled her.

"Okay, let's start," Russell said reluctantly. "Have you all had a chance to discuss this venture with your families?"

There were nods all around the table, but everyone stayed quiet.

"I'm going to be optimistic," Russell said with a half-smile. "Is there anyone who is considering *not* coming?"

No one spoke up, but no one made eye contact either. The terror in the room was palpable.

"Has anyone spoken to Tobi and Troy?" Russell continued. "I think we need them both, even though they are older. Tobi for the obvious reasons and Troy has such a wealth of information in geology and climatology, I'd hate to go without someone who can read both the planet and the weather so well."

Steve Seltzer sat up straight. "Haven't seen them, but I spoke to Greg Davidica last night, our vet. He has a lot of bitterness in him—you all know what they did to his two-year-old. But I think he's going to chance it and come. Might be just to stick it to the Whispies, but for whatever reason. His kids are excited, but his wife, Miriam, is very anxious."

"Welcome to the club," Jennifer said. "Who isn't? When are we leaving, anyway?"

Russell turned to Angelo. "No sign of further hostilities," Angelo said, "but I think the sooner we leave, the better. I do wish we could find that Sahina Keter. It makes me nervous knowing he's out there. He slips around like a shadow; I don't know how. He may have saved your life," he said, nodding to Amira, "but he was the reason you were out there to begin with. What are his intentions?"

Angie Engman, one of the engineers, put a device on the table. "This is what he was using in the field. We thought he was using it as a homing device to draw the GGP to us, but it's not anything of the sort. It's actually a signal jammer that projects data elsewhere. By using it, he probably saved us all. The planes couldn't get a bearing when they got close and then their tracking was directed west, so they flew off course and straight into the oncoming storm." She shrugged. "That doesn't explain why he won't show himself."

"Who is tallying the count of who's coming?" Russell asked.

"Troy," Ricardo answered.

"Good. Make sure he includes himself and Tobi." Russell grinned and stood up. "I think we should plan for the day after tomorrow. Teresa, is time of departure a factor for our course layout?"

Teresa chuckled. "Couldn't say. We are going to be traveling so far, I can't see it making a difference. At five times the speed of light, the trip will take roughly six weeks to get to Kepler 186f in the Cygnus system, and that's the closest choice; in the absence of other confirmed parameters, we figured it was our best bet. Departure from Earth will be more dependent on weather conditions. And we can't initiate the soliton warp until we are outside the Earth's exosphere." She looked around seriously. "We better hope the *Phoenix*'s shields hold. We cannot remain invisible, even with the stealth adaptations. There will be too much atmospheric disturbance to mask."

"Won't that expose the complex and everyone left behind?" Joshua asked timidly.

"I'm afraid it will," Jennifer answered. "We are hoping the GGP will assume that everyone is gone."

"Maybe we can use this little gadget Keter left behind to throw the GGP off course," Angie suggested.

"That would be a boon, for sure," Russell said. "See if you can figure out how to do that. We will plan for 1800 hours, day after tomorrow. That gives us nearly three days to prepare."

They all got up and straggled toward the door. Russell walked out last with Braelyn and Teresa into an otherwise empty hallway, when none other than the mysterious Sahina Keter appeared in front of them, looking furious.

The three came up short, but before they could speak, Keter, looking 100 percent male, jabbed his index finger painfully onto Russell's chest. "You broke your promise," he said.

"What?"

Keter's eyes burned into Russell with a bloodcurdling intensity that made Russell flinch and his skin crawl.

Braelyn started backing up surreptitiously toward a wall panel about four feet away where there was an alarm button.

Keter ignored Braelyn and Teresa completely and spoke only to Russell, almost like he was speaking directly into Russell's mind.

"You made a promise as the precondition of having this safe haven. You broke it. Why?"

Fatigue and confusion mixed with fear washed over Russell. He had never met this man before, and yet—there was something strangely familiar about him. "What promise?"

"Don't play dumb. The promise you made to Horatius. In exchange for the defense system. And have you not noticed how your very acreage here has multiplied? How your crops have flourished? How protected you have been for *twelve years*? Do you think that happened by accident? We never took you for an ungrateful fool, Mr. Vaderman. You were Chosen. You were told of this. Explain yourself."

Russell flashed back over a decade to the man Harris, who had rescued Russell from death at the hands of the NSA. Images he could not repel rushed through his mind. *El Curandero Grande*, saying that he, Russell, was *chosen* like a few in every generation, and that he, Russell, had been "activated."

The visage of the shaman floated before Russell's face, with blind, white eyes that saw right through him, paper-thin skin, and the long silver beard. Like a slap, Russell was immobilized. His feet would not obey him, just like the little three-year-old Russell's feet would not obey but had moved inexorably forward to stand in *El Curandero's* presence, so long ago in the Northern Peruvian Andes. And the image was nodding at him now, but not in a kind way. This time, the shaman was angry. Russell didn't know what to say.

Russell tried to look over at Braelyn but found his head was as riveted as his feet, and out of the corner of his eye, he noticed that Braelyn didn't seem to be able to move either. It was like time had just stopped for them both. Only Teresa seemed relatively free, but she didn't have a clue what was going on.

"What… what do you want me to do?" Russell's voice was quiet and hoarse. He no longer wondered how this man had passed through the complex like a shadow. No longer questioned why his intentions were unknown. And he had no illusions of being able to lock Keter up or send him away. This was beyond him. But at least he might receive some direction now.

Keter's eyes felt like they were carving a fissure into Russell's brain. "You must personally vouch for every person who embarks on this journey. You must look into their souls and use the talent you were given to determine whether their hearts are worthy of being saved." Keter paused and turned to Braelyn.

"You will assist him. You have been mostly successful in transmuting your anger, and you have developed your spirit." Keter looked back at Russell. "The torch will be passed to your sister."

"I don't want it," Braelyn said. "Forget it."

Keter looked right into her, and she flinched. "It is not your choice."

"What torch? What are you talking about?" Teresa tried to insert herself between Keter and Braelyn. Keter looked her over intensely, squinting as he did so, and seemed to have the effect of immobilizing Teresa as well. Finally, he nodded.

"You have potential. We shall see." He turned back to Russell and Braelyn. "Now, get to work. Your time is limited. We will hold the assault back for a few more days, but then you will be in grave danger."

Sahina Keter spun on his heel and disappeared around a corner in the hall, and Russell knew he would not find him if he followed.

Teresa's face was one big question mark. Russell swallowed hard and tried to explain to Teresa as briefly as he could while still trying to make some sense of it for her. A difficult task, since even after all these years, he still wasn't sure it made sense to himself. For the first time he could remember, he found himself intimidated by someone with a more highly evolved intellect.

How could he tell a mastermind scientist like Teresa about a childhood encounter with a shaman in South America and the subsequent sequalae of that encounter as an adult being threatened by the NSA? By telling her he had made promises to some character who had plucked him away from the fingers of death, wouldn't he sound like an utter idiot? Tentatively, he told her of the family vacation that was rerouted to Peoria, and Braelyn stepped in and added details when she saw him struggling. Russell could feel Braelyn's anger and discomfort regarding the references that Keter had made to herself.

Twelve years ago, the shaman had spoken of Braelyn's gift as being powerful, but said she was too full of rage to be helpful to humanity. Braelyn's anger had gradually subsided once Russell was able to show her how to order her mind so that what seemed like chaos ceased to terrify her, and she began to use her intuition as a tool. The depths of her spirit were no longer anathema to her. Keter was right about that. Braelyn now had a powerful, reasonably disciplined mind.

"I don't want any torch," Braelyn said again. "If that—that—*thing* expects me to roll over and fulfill some sort of prophecy, it's mistaken. I'm just me. I've barely gotten a handle on keeping myself from going off the deep end. I'm *comfortable* now. Don't give me anything else, or I swear, Russell—"

"Easy, Brae," Russell said. "Let's just focus on getting our traveler list together. Will you help me with interviews? Looking into someone's intentions is something you already do, sometimes, when it's really important. Let's get off the planet and we can figure it out later, okay? I can't do this by myself, there's too many people for me to evaluate in a couple of days. I need your help right now."

Russell rarely asked for help, and Braelyn was visibly moved. "All right, bro. Just this once. It's not easy to do that, though, it takes a lot of psychic energy."

"No kidding," Russell answered.

"Is this man planning to accompany us?" Teresa asked.

"No clue," Russell said. "But I can't argue that we have limited time. Those planes were a warning, and it does look like he saved us; he absolutely saved Amira. And truly, it is something of a miracle that we have survived this long without being detected. I'm not going to dispute his statement. If he wants to come, I don't see how we can refuse."

"What if he subverts the *Phoenix*? Can we trust him?" Teresa pressed.

"Why would he bring us so far just to destroy us? No, I'd be more inclined to think he may try to ensure safe passage. Harris seemed wholly motivated by the survival of humanity."

Teresa shook her head. "What is he then, some sort of god?"

Braelyn had become suddenly quiet and drawn into herself. "No," she said, as if looking at something deep within. "He is a manifestation of Spirit."

CHAPTER 33

John rode more leisurely up the highway, ambivalent about what to do next. After a half hour, he looked up and saw a small jet overhead as it flew past him to the north. After twenty seconds, he heard the wine of the missile, even though he could barely see it, then the explosion. He saw the smoke on the horizon and imagined that was the end of Jansen. Of course he would have been tagged with a transmitter, and someone at the White House had no doubt heard their whole exchange. John racked his memory trying to recall if he, himself, had said anything self-incriminating. He certainly hadn't defended the GGP. At least Jansen had met death on his own terms. Would John do the same?

He slowed further and started to search his clothes covertly, then more fervently. Were they watching him too? He must also be tagged, and he couldn't make any progress off-mission without finding the bug and ditching it. He went through his pockets, then started pressing on seams of his clothing. Maybe something was sewn into his clothes, but it was hard to do an effective search while he was riding.

He thought back to the morning of the day they left. He'd been handed these camouflage fatigues; it was easy to imagine they were bugged. John turned off at an exit that had once led into a township. He cruised unhurriedly through the neighborhood, now deserted like everywhere else, and looked into a few shops in one of the strip malls. The glass windows were shattered, and the shelves were empty.

John got off his bike and walked into a few of the stores. He was, after all, supposed to be looking for lost operatives, right? He found the body of someone who was once probably a store owner, lying on the floor in a patch of dried blood and broken glass.

He went to the man, lying inert on the floor. The wind had blown leaves and assorted trash inside, and the air was crisp and cool.

John kept staring at the corpse. Could he do this? It turned his stomach… Finally, he took a deep breath and carefully removed the man's clothes from his lifeless body, then stripped himself of his own fatigues. He looked at his underwear, and after another moment of gathering his courage, took off his briefs and his T-shirt as well. He donned the other man's clothing, dried blood and all.

He still felt vulnerable and looked suddenly at the crease inside his right elbow. There had been an annoying irritation under his skin since just before they'd left, but with all the other stresses, he had ignored it. Now he looked more carefully.

He found a mostly healed wound, very tiny, and if he pressed on it, it felt like there was a splinter there. Strange place to get a splinter. John fished around in his pack and pulled out a small knife and the first aid kit. Cleaning the knife and his skin with alcohol, he took the knife in his left hand.

They forgot I'm left-handed, he thought. Gingerly, he extended his elbow all the way and inserted the tip of the knife under his skin until it scraped against something thin and metallic. There was definitely something embedded there. He desperately wished he could use both hands, but he made the incision larger and then put the knife aside and dug in with his fingers to grab it. He wasn't even sure what he was grasping. It took the better part of an hour, and John was in a cold sweat by the time he was done, but ultimately, he held a half centimeter chip in his left fingers, and there was a pool of blood on the ground.

Washing his hand and the wound with alcohol again, he used the last of the first aid kit to apply a tight gauze dressing and leaned back against the counter to relax for a minute. His pack would have to be left behind as well.

It hadn't consciously registered in John's head yet, but apparently, he was orchestrating his own escape. Where would he go? If he found the rebels, he had no such victim story to tell them that might convince them he was no longer loyal to the GGP. He just knew they did not expect him to return from this mission alive. Unstated as it was, this was to be John's sacrifice to the Great Ganaffe Party. End of story. But John wasn't feeling that noble.

He grabbed for the power bar before abandoning his pack and supplies, then thought better of eating anything they had provided. He wandered through the little strip mall and did not find any food, but another casualty was lying on the floor and still wearing a deep blue Harrington jacket. John appropriated it almost without a thought and turned back to his bike.

Was the bike tagged? Probably. And as soon as he left the area, if he traveled with some—but not all—of the transmitters, they'd know he had mutinied. No, he had to leave the bike behind. He had to leave *everything* behind. And he had committed himself as soon as he had removed the subdermal tracer. He should have thought this through better.

There were some cars in the parking lot in various states of disrepair and vandalism. John searched the pockets of his new jacket for keys, but they were empty. Wandering to the back of the shops, a kid's scooter was lying against the concrete. It looked like it had been left recently, like maybe the kid was still around somewhere, searching through the clutter for something to eat or use.

But everything looked deserted. John ran back to his pack to take his knife with him—that had to be safe, right? Then he mounted the scooter and rode off down the street. If he could find the Appalachian Trail, maybe *he* could live off the land, in the caves near streams as Jansen had thought to do. He might have possibly brought some of the firearms, but there was no guarantee he couldn't be found that way.

As he drove further and further from his supplies and his motorcycle, his arm throbbed and his stomach growled. He felt like a little kid who had run away from home. Funny, he had none of the feeling of excitement and freedom that Jansen had experienced. The little kid analogy stayed with him. But little kids could go home for supper, and John had just sealed himself to a different fate. Different and entirely terrifying.

CHAPTER 34

By noon, the survey responses were mostly in. The number voting to leave Earth leveled at 1,543 people, and many of those were small children. No one knew how faster-than-light travel might affect children—or grown adults, for that matter—but it made no difference. To leave could put them in peril but to stay would certainly risk their lives.

They seemed to have an even assortment of skills among the group, those with knowledge of farming, carpentry, engineering, medicine, climatology, geology, even the manufacture of cosmetics. As one of the chemists pointed out, depending on the new environment, they might require skin creams to protect from the sun or an overly dry climate. And they were bringing with them a vast digital library so that the processes for fabrication of essentials of all kinds could be learned. It was crucial that they land on a planet with ample plant life that would support not only food, but manufacturing of clothing, shampoos, lubricants, rope, and building materials. Fortunately, they had a botanist.

Claire hadn't come to them as a botanist. She was only eighteen when she arrived; her family was butchered while she was away at school, and she feared to stay at her university. She left as a freshman with her major still undecided and found her way to what seemed to be the only safe place on the East Coast. She chose to study botany in the community because she felt it would be useful, and she chased down information so enthusiastically that Russell had told her he wished he could confer upon her a PhD. It was her way of fleeing the ghosts from her past.

Living in isolation, the community had learned to produce most of what it needed and to make do with less than they were previously used to. The former sense of privilege and entitlement that had characterized much of America had disintegrated when faced with the Whispies' brutal attacks and the average person's sudden recognition of the need for only the raw elements of survival. No one complained that their favorite breakfast cereal was no longer on the menu. Every single inhabitant of the complex was just grateful to be alive, and most considered themselves lucky to have more than they needed.

As plans were being made for departure, as far back as months ago, it was discussed and they had resolved not to take any animals. But in the end, they decided to bring the wolves. First, they had become like family, were highly intelligent, and Braelyn could effectively communicate with them to keep them on a mental leash—at least here in their familiar surroundings— and second, they might be useful as protection. What they would eat, being carnivores, how they would react to strange life forms, and how they might upset the ecosystem of an unknown planet were major concerns. But one could say that held equally true for humans engaging in life on a world where they had not evolved.

As near as they could predict, weather conditions would be adequate to schedule liftoff in two days' time. Russell and Braelyn requested that everyone wishing to make the journey report by noon the next day with their belongings, which were limited to essential items and clothing that could fit in a single valise. Once aboard the *Phoenix*, they were not to disembark again.

They made an announcement that their numbers were slightly above capacity and gave the choice to draw lots to eliminate the overflow or simply add more people to a room in some cases. This would make for less comfortable accommodations, but it was almost unanimously agreed to, since drawing lots might mean being left behind. Russell thought it also spoke volumes for the goodwill of the passengers.

As directed, Russell and Braelyn interviewed everyone as they boarded. They needed to inventory who was coming, their ages, their skill sets, and their state of health anyway. It was a solemn task, as people stepped onto the ship and said goodbye to the Earth forever. A few musical instruments were approved, even though they were oversized, if the owners promised to provide music to all.

Russell was pleased to see the veterinarian, Greg Davidica, coming aboard with his wife, Miriam, his daughter, Anna, and his son, Caleb. He was carrying a large extra bag with medical instruments and supplies. Russell glanced in routinely and approved it.

"I'm glad you're coming," he said. "We need you. You

will be a true asset to the community, perhaps one of the most essential."

Greg nodded, and as they passed the threshold, little Anna ducked her head and hid on the other side of her father. She was carrying a soft fabric case that was fairly large for a nine-year-old.

"What'ya got there?" Russell asked.

She looked panic stricken and hid behind her father. Russell squatted down in front of her and heard a faint but distinct meow emanating from the pack.

"Sweetheart, do you have a cat in there?"

Anna looked at her father who nodded to her with a frown, and then looked timidly up at Russell. "Yes," she said, so quietly it was nearly inaudible.

This was the part Russell hated. "I'm sorry, sweetie, we can't take animals with us."

"But he'll die here! I can't leave him. I won't. I won't go without Micky!"

Russell looked at Greg for help, but Greg shook his head. "She's been through so much. That cat is the only thing that's gotten her to smile since her baby sister…since Alana was murdered. I won't separate them."

Russell stood up and the two men faced each other. He didn't know what to say. He was beyond annoyed that Greg had tried to get the animal onboard through deception. But the determination on Greg's face spoke volumes. He was not giving in on this. Would he actually keep his family behind for a cat? Or was he banking on how much they needed his expertise?

Braelyn was only a few feet away and she came over to

help out. She put her hand on Anna's head and asked to look at the kitty.

"No! You'll take him away," Anna yelled.

"Come talk over here," Braelyn said to the Davidicas, and removed them from the line and the eyesight of the other passengers. To Russell she said, "I'll take care of it."

Russell was relieved and went back to interviewing the rest of the travelers.

"What kind of kitty is he?" Braelyn asked.

Anna just shrugged, but Greg answered for her.

"He's a Maine Coon, mostly, anyway. They're extremely smart and trainable. He's about five or six years old, and he came to Anna and basically claimed her. He sleeps with her, he follows her, he sits in her lap. It's as if he knows how much she needs him. You know… when she was only four, she watched her sister tortured and killed. She wouldn't speak a word to anyone for over a year. Please, she *needs* her cat. And the cat seems to know it." There were tears in Greg's eyes, and Braelyn struggled to hold back her own. She looked at the little girl for a solid minute. She was slight, with long, straight, mouse-brown hair and big gray eyes. She stood there sniffling with a determined look on her face, and Braelyn got an eerie premonition that this girl and her cat were important somehow.

"Let me see Micky," Braelyn said.

Reluctantly, and without letting go of the carrier, Anna opened the zipper a couple of inches and Braelyn looked in. Staring right back at her was a rather large cat, but Braelyn had never seen an animal that looked like this. It was shades of dark brown in a tabby pattern, with a face framed in long fur that looked more like a lion's than a pussycat's. Its hair was bushy and soft, and the eyes were intelligent and intense. Braelyn *reached* for it with her mind and felt instantly that Micky was fearless and loyal. It was patiently sizing Braelyn up with its attention centered on protecting the little girl. Braelyn liked the animal immediately.

Braelyn spoke to Anna very seriously. "You will be completely responsible for Micky, you understand? You must keep him fed, take care of his litter box needs, keep his claws trimmed, and make sure he doesn't tear anything apart. And *most* important: You *must* keep him quiet. Cats aren't allowed on the flight, so no one can know. Can you do that?"

Anna looked up with disbelief. She nodded her head almost violently and clutched her cat tightly through the soft carrier, which the cat tolerated rather well. Then, on impulse, she hugged Braelyn for a split second before closing the zipper and rubbing her eyes dry with the back of her fist. She stood up very straight next to her father. Braelyn thought if she knew how to salute, she might have done that as well.

"Okay, hop on board you guys, before my brother figures it out."

Greg shook her hand quickly and awkwardly, Caleb grinned and jumped aboard with a spring in his step, and Miriam took her hand for a quick, grateful squeeze. Braelyn hurriedly ushered them in; she just wanted them to get settled without drawing attention to themselves. She felt rather than saw Sahina Keter watching her and wondered if he'd have anything to say about it.

It took until 11:00 p.m. to get most everyone on board and assigned to quarters, and each had been questioned by either Russell or Braelyn. Every one of them had anger and grief bottled up inside them, appropriate reactions to the violent way they had seen loved ones die or had lost everything they had built over their lives. The people in the compound all had that one thing in common, and it bound them tightly; their lives had all been reduced to bare essentials and so many had found themselves alone. But none of them were "bad people" as far as Russell and Braelyn could determine. No one seemed motivated to go off on a blind killing spree, jeopardize their community, or injure innocent people. They were all dealing with their losses and their wrath as best as could be expected. No one was denied entry.

Some passengers found themselves with a roommate they did not know well, although as such a small community, they all pretty much had seen each other at some point or another. There was the excitement of a new adventure mixed with the fear of the unknown. Most did not consider that they might burn up on arrival or even whether they would be shot down by the government before they achieved orbit. There was an assumption that they would make it, that the people who had been planning this had all their ducks in a row. No one paid much attention to the seat belts and wall handles that had been installed in every room for passengers to hang on to if needed.

CHAPTER 35

The next morning, Teresa was on the bridge speaking intensely to the pilot, Kevin Burns. Kevin had been training on a simulator since there had been no way to take the *Phoenix* for a test run without spilling their hand, and maybe losing the ship in the process. Kevin was thirty-five and before the GGP took over, he had been an air force pilot and interested in space travel "one day." While he had logged several thousands of hours in the air, he had never experienced either the intensity of G-forces that would be generated when breaking completely out of the Earth's gravitational field or the nuances of flying in zero gravity.

Teresa had been working with him since her arrival using a technique of imaginative practice, where, in a semi meditative state, he would live the flight in his mind and respond to as many possible scenarios as possible, so that when the time came in reality to lift off and embark, it would be second nature to his subconscious self.

She was also teaching him breathing techniques to stay calm and focused, no matter what his orientation in space or the effects of gravitational forces on his body were. She had worked less intensely with the copilot, Shannon Giveners, mostly because Shannon had been more occupied with Jennifer, setting up systems and integrating the computer.

Jennifer was hovering near the Q and doing some last-minute explanation of programming to Joelle, their navigator, on how to plot a course through the computer. Devon had come up as well. He was in charge of communications for the time being and had transferred his program of universal symbols to the Q. Since it was based on the mathematics of music, employed as primary language substrates, it was fairly easy to digitize, but it still needed a lot of polishing, and, of course, it was as yet untested, but it was a start if they were confronted with any alien life early on.

Braelyn came in to look around gingerly. She looked completely out of her element, as she understood none of this, but she was the most able to project her mind, so her skills might be vital at some point, and she needed to familiarize herself with the bridge.

The room was roughly square, looking like an oversized cockpit, with consoles around the periphery and the two seats for the pilot and copilot up front in the center. The navigator's console was off to the left and a step lower than the pilots'. There was a seat beside it for the weapons and defense station. On the right hung the Q, alien and spectacular, almost glowing in its diamond-plated casing, and Jennifer had a seat adjacent to it. The communications station was behind the Q, and in the rear of the bridge were three additional seats bolted into the floor.

The front of the bridge was a huge screen, which was currently in window form so they could see who and what was in the vicinity, but it could also be converted to a camera that provided pictures of the very far away that would otherwise not be visible to the naked eye.

Russell was in the compound's security section with Angelo, evaluating a missile that had exploded twenty-three miles to the southeast. It was unclear what the target had been; on the surface, it seemed to have nothing to do with them, as after detonation, the plane had veered off back to the south and disappeared. But Russell and Angelo were both suspicious and hesitated to open the mountaintop until they were positive that there was no threat to them.

Some of the community members who elected to stay behind were in deep study of the defense systems as well as the device Sahina Keter had been using during the storm. The idea was to engage the device just as the *Phoenix* employed its thrusters and to project the disturbance *away* to keep anyone from identifying the site of the complex, even though it was hoped that the GGP would assume they were all gone. Ricardo was with another group showing them the farming equipment and the climate sensors.

At 1700, one hour prior to their scheduled departure, the cameras showed a man wandering around the base of the mountain. An alarm went off and Russell, Angelo, and a security team met to evaluate what needed to be done.

He appeared to be alone; he was wearing a blue jacket and he had no supplies. On magnification, they saw the jacket was open and his shirt underneath was bloody, but he did not walk like a man with a chest injury. There was no hesitancy of movement or labored breathing, but he was favoring his right arm. He circled an elm tree for a few minutes, and then leaned his back to it in a posture of defeat. He looked like a man beaten.

"What do we do about him?" asked Angelo.

Russell ran his hands through his hair. What a time for this! They could ignore him and he'd probably move on; he didn't seem to have discovered anything or found anything to be amiss. But in less than an hour, the ground would open up and a huge ship would lift off, and *that* would be unmistakable.

"Maybe we should bring him in and figure out what and who he is," Angelo continued, "so he can't blow the whistle on the compound. We're leaving, it won't make a difference to us if he sees us go, but what about to those left behind?"

"And if we decide he's a GGP spy, what then?" Russell asked. "Are you prepared to kill him?"

It was a question they had so far avoided having to come to terms with.

"Maybe he's another Sahina Keter," Angelo said with a sardonic laugh.

Russell shot him a withering look. "How about we ask the new head of security what she wants to do?" he suggested.

Erin was being briefed on systems, but she came up when she heard the news. "I don't know what to do," she said. "I don't want to start our new autonomy in this place with murder on our hands."

Erin had been NYPD in Brooklyn for ten years before defecting to the complex. She was no stranger to violence, and killing in self-defense was not an issue. But this would be inviting someone in and then, if they decided he didn't belong, killing him in cold blood. It was a murder that could be avoided. How was she to know what to do with this guy?

"I don't see how you can get around evaluating him personally. You can meet him in a controlled fashion, on your own terms, or wait until he sees the ship leave and he becomes a wild card. But this is your establishment now," Russell said. "This will not be your last encounter. You have to decide if you want to bring in newcomers or not, and what you will do with them if they prove to be a liability."

The man on the screen was now walking slowly toward the mountainside, looking lost and even frightened. He finally put his face against the trunk of a maple tree and his hands on a branch above his head and stayed motionless. Whether he was praying or waiting for something more worldly was unclear, but leaving him there did not seem to be the best option. The clock was ticking.

Erin nodded with resignation. "Let's bring him in then. If he found us, others will too. Maybe he needs sanctuary. We have lots of room now." She gave them a half smile.

When the mountainside shifted to open the gate, the man nearly jumped out of his skin. Several armed men quickly grabbed him and pulled him inside, confiscated his knife after searching him, and brought him before Erin, Russell, and Angelo.

"Who are you and what do you want?" Erin demanded.

The man looked nothing short of terrified.

"Answer me, damn it. Who sent you?" The man just stared, wide-eyed and speechless, and Erin lost her patience. "Give me a reason to trust you, and do it quick. Make it the truth, or you're a dead man."

The man swallowed hard and answered slowly and deliberately, measuring his words and knowing his life depended on it.

"My name is John Sentics. The GGP sent me here to die."

CHAPTER 36

John sat in something that looked like an interrogation room, or maybe it just felt that way since he was being interrogated. He had not expected to stumble onto this place at all and had not thought through what he would say or do if he did. He was immensely grateful that he had ditched the transmitters—at least the ones he could find—and that he had left his radio behind. There was no way he would have had an opportunity to send a signal, since he had no idea he had arrived, and then he was captured immediately.

How was he going to convince these people to let him live? Did he have anything to offer? John almost wished he had the physical scars that Jansen had so he could show them and prove he had no love for the GGP. But...did he actually hate them? He hadn't felt much of anything for them, just went along with whatever they said, happy to be on the fringes of the inner circle because it meant he could keep his skin a while longer, and watch dispassionately as the staff Justine hired, one by one, were sent to their demise in as useful a way as she could muster. He was not much of a patriot or a rebel. When he thought about himself that way, he was not impressed. He felt like a nobody, a man without principles just trying to survive in a world of dictatorship.

The man who had introduced himself as simply "V" sat down across from him. John got that they didn't want to trust him with their names, but V was on the ridiculous side. He almost laughed, but when the man looked at him, John lost his humor. The man said nothing, just stared at him with the most intense eyes John had ever seen.

The silence stretched out and John began to sweat. The hairs on the back of his neck stood up, and he felt a crawling sensation in his skin. He felt like his mind was being opened up and gazed upon, but he couldn't look away. The others stood in a semicircle behind V and just waited.

Finally, V broke contact and stood up. He seemed to be sweating too.

"You've been dosed with scopolamine. What were your instructions? What did you come here to do?"

John licked is lips, trying not to react to this man's perception of the drug residue on him. He certainly couldn't deny it, but how did this guy know?

"I was told to send a signal when I found you and then try to find a way in. But I ditched my radio and my clothes in a small town a few miles away. I even removed the chip they planted in my arm." They had already taken his jacket and searched it, so he rolled up his sleeve. What he saw shocked him. No wonder his arm hurt so much!

John's right inside elbow at the site of the chip removal

was swollen and red, crusted, with new vesicles forming, and there were red streaks running up toward his shoulder. He couldn't help but gasp.

"I just took that out this morning… It's been hurting, but I didn't stop to look—"

"You were obviously not supposed to remove it," the woman said. The three rebels looked at each other like they didn't know what to do with him now.

"Am I going to die from this?"

"What makes you think we will not kill you for coming here anyway?" the woman asked.

"Noth-nothing," John stuttered. "I never expected to find you. I was just running away, but had nowhere to go."

"How did you manage to overcome the scopolamine suggestion?" V asked quietly. "And why should you be given sanctuary?"

John did his best to explain, talking faster than he wanted to. *Everyone* who worked at the White House was dosed with scopolamine. But in his tier, it was a lower dose, and he had stopped eating the food recently. He told them about Jansen, how he thought the man would be a liability, but Jansen had been so abused, he defected as soon as he had the chance, and they had killed him for it. John knew no one expected to see him alive again, and he was afraid to look for his own family, as that would implicate them. He threw himself on the mercy of the rebels and then, like a prisoner expecting the guillotine, he lowered his head and waited for the blade.

————

Erin, Russell, and Angelo stepped aside to talk. The man seemed harmless and probably had a lot of information that he might not even know was useful. He could be an asset. But how could they know? The only two people with any psi skills were Russell and Braelyn, and they were both going off-world.

"Do you want to take him with you to the new planet?" Erin asked. "He can't do much harm there; he'll be too far away."

"Yes, but what if he's programmed to jam our systems or sabotage the *Phoenix* just when we start to trust him?" Angelo jumped in. "I'm not comfortable taking someone as untried and historically disloyal as this pathetic excuse for a rebel is on a journey that is already fraught with hazards. He hasn't even said he wants to help the resistance. He's only here trying to save his own skin."

"Well, isn't that why all of us, fundamentally, are here?" Russell asked.

"If you lift off and leave him behind, he could give us all away," Erin said.

Angelo stood with his arms across his chest, shaking his head. "Then kill him. If he comes, he might destroy our chances of landing anywhere, and we would die in space. I say he stays behind." He looked at Erin. "Do with him whatever you must here on Earth. But keep him *away* from the *Phoenix*."

Angelo and Russell headed back to secure final preparations for departure. Joshua was sitting on the floor just inside the ship, with his pack and travel supplies, but he had not gone to set up his quarters for the journey.

Russell went to him. "Hey, Josh, what's up? Do you need help finding your assigned living space?"

"Oh, hi Uncle Russell," Joshua said, sounding very distracted. "No, I know I'm staying with Mom—which is kind of weird, I think, considering I'm thirty-six and all." He shrugged.

"We all have to double up a little to accommodate the extra people who want to join us. I don't want to leave behind anyone who wants to come. Would you rather stay with me?"

"That's just it, Uncle, I don't understand why *anyone* wants to stay here. Like, take my friend Stephanie. She refuses to come, says she's afraid for her little boy in space. He's only six. I told her there were lots of kids coming, but she says she won't chance it. But Uncle Russell—they'll die here! Don't they see that?"

Russell took Joshua by the elbow and led him to a small room off the entryway and invited him to sit.

"Josh, some people just prefer the 'devil they know' to the one they don't know. She's afraid."

"Geez, Uncle, I know that! I'm not a stupid little kid anymore. But why would she stay and face certain death when there's a chance for life out there?" Joshua's arm swept the air in a wide arc.

Russell recoiled at Joshua's outburst. Gone were the days when his nephew was too intimidated by the world and too simplistic to understand people and events to do other than pad along after his mother, aunt, and uncle. Fatigue welled up in him.

"Is Stephanie the girl you were dating?"

Joshua's face colored. "Yeah, sort of. I guess so. And I'm

afraid for her. And…and I'm going to *miss* her. And I can't even get her to understand what I'm saying! She keeps thinking maybe it will all be all right, as if the encampment can stay hidden forever. I told her about the planes and the bomb and everything."

Joshua looked like he was going to cry, and Russell leaned forward and took his hand. "Most people only see what they're ready to see. If their minds are closed, nothing gets in. Doesn't matter how much sense it makes."

"But, Uncle, you always taught me to examine everything. Not to make assumptions, and to think things out with my head. I love our planet Earth, but it doesn't make any *sense* to stay here now."

Russell leaned over and hugged his nephew. "Not to you, not to me. But we can't control other people."

"I'm afraid she'll regret it right after we lift off, and then it will be too late," Joshua said, hanging his head.

Russell squeezed Joshua once more and let him go. "Let's see where you're assigned." He pulled a copy of the roster off the wall and perused it quickly.

"Looks like you're not with mom anymore. She's with Teresa Simmons and Amira. You're sharing with Devon and another boy, Montrose. Do you know him?"

"Oh yeah, Monty. He's a wiz at growing crops and things, but he also created the greenhouse and little botanical gardens. He's real sad to leave them behind."

"Hmm. Your room shows four beds. Who's the fourth?" Russell asked.

"I don't know. Maybe it's someone invisible, like that guy Sahina Keter," Joshua said and burst out laughing.

A shiver ran up Russell's spine.

CHAPTER 37

They were assembled on the bridge. Jennifer was monitoring the Q, Kevin and Shannon were up front in the pilot and copilot seats, and Joelle was at her navigation console on the right. Erika, who had handled security cameras in the encampment had chosen to come and had received a crash course on the ship's monitoring systems. This also put her in charge of weapons, a role she was not very enthusiastic about. Devon sat at the communications console behind Jennifer, and Teresa was in a seat at the rear of the cockpit, looking like she'd rather be pacing than strapped in with a seat belt.

They had the coordinates of the Cygnus star system programmed into the Q, as that held the closest potential planet, but first they had to break out of the Earth's atmosphere and attain orbit. Otherwise, the force of the creation of the soliton would produce such a storm behind them, it could put a hole in the Catskills Mountains that might extend all the way to the Atlantic Ocean. It was not their intention to destroy anything; simply to leave in peace.

Russell and Braelyn took seats at the rear next to Teresa. The tension in the air was palpable and for the first three minutes, no one spoke at all. Just shuffled in their seats, readying their controls, and waiting for a signal. Russell had been the *de facto* leader on the ground, but he knew next to nothing about flying a space vessel. While all eyes and ears were on Russell, Russell was waiting for a cue from Kevin.

Finally, Russell made it official. He got on the intercom and spoke to the entire ship.

"Everyone should be in their assigned quarters and strapped into seats. Your seats all recline, and you should be in that reclined position with the seats locked, so you are basically lying flat on the floor. This is so the G forces we will be pulling will not cause you to pass out. Once we are out of the Earth's orbit and cruising through the solar system and into outer space, you will be able to get up and move about, and there are several observation decks throughout the ship. From this point on, the commander of our expedition is Captain Kevin Burns, assisted by his associate and copilot, Captain Shannon Giveners. We will embark on his word."

Russell nodded to Kevin who nodded back and took a deep breath.

Kevin looked to Devon and asked him to open the communication channel to the compound. "Erin, do you read me?"

"Loud and clear, Captain," came Erin's voice.

"Are you ready with the signal jammer?"

"Good to go," Erin said.

Kevin looked uncomfortable for a moment. "Then, this is

it, my friend. It's been a true privilege. May all of our lives be long and unfettered, and perhaps we will meet again one day in better times." He took a deep breath. "Please open the mountain canopy. We are about to initiate thrusters."

"Best of luck to you," Erin said.

Kevin nodded to Joelle. The bridge itself rotated to recline their seats with their consoles so the blood would not rush from their heads upon launch.

And then it seemed to take no time at all. The "ceiling" that had hidden the *Phoenix* for so long swiveled and slid to the side. Until that moment, the ship had been neatly tucked away in the mountain, blending into the west side of the canyon like an irregularity of the rock face. Within a couple of minutes, the sky above was clearly visible, and the top of the ship gleamed as the fading sunlight swept across it. The *Phoenix* began to arc into the sky almost immediately.

The starship was sleek and graceful looking, like a vastly oversized bullet with a large belly. There were retractable wings that were used only when in the atmosphere, and once they attained orbit, Shannon would withdraw them into the hull. There was a heat shield that could be deployed on reentry but was currently hidden, and the modified *Inconel*® hull shimmered with a soft silver glow and a symbol of a majestic bird on each side.

On the bridge, there were two sets of cameras in front of them, one directed toward the front and one showing the rear view. It was awe-inspiring to see the mountaintop askew and then moving slowly back to replace its usual position, as if it had never budged. The process took about two minutes. By the time it was fully retracted, looking just like an ordinary mountainside, the *Phoenix* was into the stratosphere and the Catskills had been lost from view.

"Any sign of pursuit?" Kevin asked Erika, struggling to speak while his cheeks were pulled back against his ears.

"None. I hardly believe it. Either we took them completely by surprise or they have no idea we exist," Erika said.

"Oh, they know we exist, at least they do now," Shannon said. "They must see us. Stay vigilant; they just need time to organize a chase this high in the atmosphere. Their supersonic fighter planes are fast, but they can't fly this high. The timing of our departure does not bring us particularly close to any of the orbiting space stations, but there are four of them evenly placed around the planet's circumference. And those are just the Americans. I wouldn't rest easy until we're out of the Earth's orbit and initiate the soliton warp."

Russell had an impulse to bark orders, but he bit his lip. He had appropriately relinquished his leadership role to the pilot of this ship, but the habit was hard to break. As frustrating as it was, he had to let Captains Burns and Giveners take it from here. They knew where they were going.

The Earth looked just like they used to see in photos taken from the space station. A bluish globe with white swirls of clouds covering much of it in an irregular pattern. At this distance, the great warps in the crust and the fires over the land were erased, and their world looked pure and undefiled. As they passed out of what Kevin called the magnetosphere, the fifth and outermost layer of the Earth's atmosphere, the gravitational force on their bodies lessened, and the bridge rotated back toward its original position. It was easier to breathe. But in that instant, Erika sounded an alarm.

"There are ships approaching from our starboard side,"

she said. "I do not know what their weapons capabilities are, if any… wait, I'm getting a reading…"

"I thought we can determine that. We can evaluate weapons on planes on Earth, right?" Shannon asked.

"Information is coming in and Q is analyzing," Jennifer said, "but we don't have a large database on what the warships in space look like."

"Why the hell not?" Shannon said.

"Simple," Jennifer answered. "We used to have an Outer Space Treaty, an international arms agreement barring weapons of mass destruction from orbit. That was before Ganaffe and the GGP took power. There was always a suspicion that the Russians had ignored the treaty, but it has never been common knowledge what those systems look like. Even Iran launched a missile reconnaissance satellite about fifteen years ago; that's a fancy way of saying a missile that destroys satellites. Some of the havoc that's been played on our internet has come from these interceptors— it's not all from the GGP. There's no actual data, but I wouldn't put it past those ships coming at us as having a nuclear arsenal. Whether they can accurately fire at another ship or are more designed to aim at the planet below, is anyone's guess."

"How long until we can engage the soliton?" Russell could contain himself no longer.

"The soliton is charging," Kevin answered, "has been since we lifted off. It will be another five to six minutes before it is ready to initiate."

"Five to six minutes is a long time," Devon said under his breath.

"Increasing to full non-warp speed," Kevin said. "We

have more power at our fingertips than they do, we should be able to outrun them even without the warp."

Indeed, they seemed to be pulling away. As it became clear that the ships that had come from the space station were losing ground, three missiles were launched at them.

"Evasive action," Kevin said calmly. "Bearing hard to port. Erika, raise our shields."

"Copy. Shields up. The missiles are turning with us," Erika reported. "They must be heat seeking or are being controlled remotely by the mother ship."

"What is the expected maximum speed of the missiles?" Shannon asked.

"Unknown," Jennifer said, as her eyes flew over the Q's screen.

"Can we shoot them down?" Kevin asked.

Erika was focused on her console. "I'm engaging our laser weapons," she said. "Okay, I have a fix."

"Fire when ready," Kevin said.

There was a bright flash off their starboard side.

"Got it!" Erika said.

They all started cheering.

"Whoa," Kevin broke in, "that was one of three. We're not done yet."

A couple of minutes passed as the *Phoenix* turned several times, often sharply, which was unnerving, and the laser flashed again, followed by another bright flare as the second missile disintegrated.

The third missile seemed to be adopting an evasive action of its own, despite its mother ship being nowhere in sight. As it came alongside the *Phoenix*, it blew up, and the shock wave rocked their ship, but just as it exploded and before there was impact with any flying debris, the soliton warp engaged. The *Phoenix* just disappeared from orbit. The passengers felt a sudden, surreal sensation of floating and flying at the same time, like entering a tunnel of zero gravity where everything was a blur, but nothing moved.

The cameras showing the outside of the ship abruptly had nothing to focus on and went gray. No one was prepared for the disorienting effect of the speed. It was hard to *think*.

All over the ship, passengers felt the jolt. Some clamped their eyes closed and cupped their ears with their hands, as if trying to shut out something external to themselves, but they were unsuccessful. Some cried out. The overpoweringly disorienting sensation was coming from *inside* themselves. Like being on a roller coaster from the inside out, and it could not be compensated for. It seemed to last forever.

Russell came to himself first, not a surprise since when his mind had been altered as a babe, he had learned to organize his thoughts around massive information dumps as a matter of survival. He opened his eyes and found himself panting, trying to catch his breath, yet he had not moved a centimeter in his seat.

Braelyn came around next, using the mental discipline she had learned from Russell. They met each other's eyes, incapable of speech for the first few minutes. They were the only two who didn't have their eyes squeezed shut and who weren't gripping their chairs with such a force that their knuckles were white—even though there was no relative motion of anyone on deck.

Russell recognized how dangerous this was; the pilot and navigator had been blinded. He unstrapped himself gingerly, expecting to be thrown across the bridge, but the ship could have been stationary and docked in port for all the resistance he encountered. He stood up slowly and walked over to Kevin.

Gripping the back of Kevin's chair, as if he still expected to slide across the room, he shook Kevin's shoulder gently. Braelyn did the same, inching her way cautiously over to Joelle. Since Kevin had been unresponsive, Braelyn didn't waste time with physical touch and instead *reached* into Joelle's mind and nudged it gently. *Wake up, open your eyes. We need you out here.* Joelle's head turned a little and her face relaxed, but her eyes stayed closed for another half a minute.

Seeing the change in Joelle's face, Russell did the same with Kevin, and the pilot opened his eyes. Everyone else's face was white, but color started to come back into Russell's and Braelyn's, especially now that their pilot and navigator were conscious again. Teresa managed to shake herself awake as well and went immediately to Devon, placing her hands on his temples until he opened his eyes. It looked like something she had done many times in the past.

Jennifer literally shook herself out, moving her head back and forth, and moaning until she could open her eyes, which left Shannon locked in that state, her face looking like a portrait of *The Scream*. She and Erika took the longest to come around, and Erika had dry heaves as soon as she did.

Erika was the first to speak. "Well, I'm glad I didn't eat before we left."

Teresa was leaning over the navigation console and reading the speedometer. She spoke almost in a whisper.

"We did it. We are traveling at 186,000 miles per second. The speed of light."

CHAPTER 38

All over the ship, passengers were in various states of consciousness and panic. No one had warned them what to expect. No one had even considered what it might feel like. The old science fiction television shows that portrayed ships zipping around the universe at warp speeds had never described anything like this.

Many who were able made their way to the sick bay, thinking something was desperately wrong. Tobi Lister was still immobile and trying to shake off the effects, her partner, Troy, beside her. He had weathered it better and was soothing her with cool compresses to her forehead. But the room was filling up quickly, and there was nowhere to put people. And there was nothing specifically wrong with them either, they just felt awful.

Tobi's protégé was younger and had recovered more quickly. His name was Simon, and he had completed two years in an emergency medicine residency before defecting and coming to the Catskills encampment, but he had been working with them for the last several years. He tried to reassure everyone that what they were feeling was probably normal and that it seemed as if it would pass on its own. Finally, in desperation, he signaled the bridge and asked for a general announcement to be made.

On the bridge, Kevin looked at Russell with puzzlement. He knew how to fly a plane, and—apparently—a spaceship, but he did not know how to comfort all these passengers who were now his charge. "Would you? Everyone knows your voice, they trust you."

Russell took the comm and cleared his throat.

"May I have everyone's attention. I know that transition was a shock. None of us had any idea what shifting to light speed travel would feel like and we were all unprepared. But let me reassure you, the effects seem transient, and there shouldn't be any lasting problems. Please do not crowd the sick bay unless you have another, unrelated medical problem." He handed the comm back to Kevin and nodded for him to continue.

"This...this is Captain Burns. We have successfully attained warp speed and we are now traveling at the speed of light. No one has ever accomplished this before; we are on uncharted ground—or...path." He stumbled over the euphemism. "We will need to increase speed in order to reach our target galaxy in a few weeks' time rather than spending months in space, but we will keep the velocity constant for now so we can all adjust, and we'll try to anticipate what the effects of even faster travel might mean."

He turned off the comm and looked from Russell to Teresa to Jennifer. "What *will* increasing speed mean for us?" Just then, a soft alert went off on the Q and was answered immediately and automatically by Joelle's navigation system.

"What was that?" Shannon asked.

Jennifer had a big grin on her face, the first since liftoff.

"*That*, my friend, was Q detecting a star on the horizon 0.02 parsecs away and activating the navigational system to plot and initiate a course around it." Jennifer looked as proud as a new mother.

"Oh," Shannon said, her face turning white again.

"It only activates if we are in a dead-on course for the star. Even at the speed of light, the solar gravity might affect our speed or pull us off course. Better to make a planned course change. And of course, we don't need any collisions, light speed or otherwise," Jennifer continued.

Kevin cleared his throat. "So this sensation will be worse when we jump to five times light speed, won't it? That's the speed we calculated for arrival in three weeks and five days. We don't have a lot of extra food to take us beyond that. I mean, we have the botanical garden, but that's to provide essential nutrients, it was never intended to deliver needed calories to the entire ship's detail."

"It might, or it might be easier," Teresa said. "When the brain encounters something completely *other*, something it does not know how to understand, it is overwhelmed. Once we've all had the experience, having another similar one may be much easier to process. In short, yes, it might be exponentially worse. But it also might be just a fleeting moment of disorientation as our brains categorize the sensation as something now familiar."

"Let's hope for that," Joelle said. "So is the ship now on something like autopilot?"

"Q is flying this ship, yes," Jennifer said. "If you want to take over manual control, it's highly advised that we break out of warp to do so. Our human reflexes cannot respond appropriately to anything we encounter at this speed."

In the sick bay, Simon had convinced most passengers that they were just feeling the effects of the "turbulence" and could go back to their rooms. A few still felt nauseated but oddly, no one had actually vomited. One little girl was standing quietly to the side with a cloth carry case.

Simon walked over to her. "What'ya got there, sweetie?"

"I'm not supposed to show anyone, but you're a doctor, right?"

Simon squatted down. "Yes, I am. Do you need help? Do you…is there *someone* in there who needs help?"

The little girl shook her head determinedly. "My daddy's a vet. if Micky needed help, I'd go to him."

Simon looked puzzled. "Okay, did you just come to visit?"

"Of course not! But Micky figured it out. I thought you should know, to help the others. But you can't tell *anyone* about Micky. Doctors are supposed to keep confidences, right? So I think I can tell you."

More perplexed than ever and feeling weary and not quite adjusted to what had happened himself, Simon stood up and walked over to a chair beside one of the beds.

"Can you tell me over here? I need to sit down. Maybe you do too. What's your name?"

"I don't need to sit down. I'm fine. Because of Micky. He can help you. You can't tell *anybody* though."

"Okay, I won't tell anyone. What's your name?"

"My name is Anna. And this is Micky." She unzipped the

carrier a few inches and Simon saw the head of what looked at first to be a miniature lion. He jumped back.

"He won't hurt you," Anna said. "Not unless you hurt *me*."

"I would never hurt you, Anna."

"I know." Anna sat down on the floor, fully confident now. She opened the carrier the rest of the way and pulled out an enormous cat and held it in her lap. The cat was completely docile and let the girl move him any way she chose. But when Simon leaned over toward them, its hair instantly stood up on end and it gave a sharp hiss.

"You can't make any sudden movements, and you have to ask permission to come close," Anna said. "That's just how he is. Even my daddy learned he has to ask permission. Then if Micky likes you, he'll say okay."

Simon wasn't sure if he were more amused or surprised by this, but his general discomfort after the warp engagement was starting to fade away. He addressed the cat.

"How do you do, Micky? Is it okay if I come a little closer?"

Micky turned away as if ignoring Simon but did not react as Simon moved closer. No hissing or snarling, it was almost as if the cat no longer realized he was there.

"Anna, why did you bring Micky here? You could get in trouble if some people found out that you have a cat on board."

"I know. That's why you mustn't tell. But everyone was feeling so horrible after we left Earth, and doctors have to be at their best. I wanted Micky to help you like he helped me and my family. Look…"

Anna crooned softly to the cat and picked him up by the

shoulders, dragging him over to Simon. "Just put him in your lap for a second. You'll see."

Simon eyed the little girl like she was fantasizing, but since he liked cats and missed his own, he complied. "Micky," he said very seriously, "may I put you in my lap?"

Micky looked at the doctor and if cats could shrug, it seemed he would have. Simon gently lifted the cat and put him on his lap. He must have weighed fifteen pounds or more.

As soon as Micky settled, he started to purr. The most remarkable sensation vibrated through Simon. After a few seconds, his brain and his body were united again, and he realized that was what had felt off before, in some bizarre way. It was almost as though the vibration of the cat's purring had knitted the parts of himself back together. He gave a profound sigh of relief, and he didn't know what to say.

"You see?" little Anna said. "Micky fixes it."

"Indeed, he does. Hey, do you think Micky—" He turned to the cat instead. "Micky, do you think you could help our other doctor as well? She's having a hard time coming back to herself. She's a little older, maybe that's the problem."

The cat stared at Simon and Simon felt like the creature was speaking plainly only he, the idiot human, could not understand. He stood up to gently carry the cat over to Tobi, but Micky jumped down in distaste and trotted over to Tobi on his own.

"He said you could put him in your lap, he didn't say you could *take* him anywhere," Anna scolded.

Tobi was lying on one of the sick bay beds with the back elevated and holding Troy's hand. Her eyes were open, and she looked a little better than she had ten minutes ago.

Before Simon could say anything, Tobi shook her head. "I'm fine, Simon, really. It'll just take a few more minutes and I'll be okay."

Micky leaped up on the gurney.

"Oh! A cat." Tobi jumped.

But the cat ignored her surprise and put a big paw on Tobi's chest, then lay down across her. The purring started and Tobi was in too much shock to say anything. Reflexively, she started stroking the cat, and the purring got louder. She looked down at the creature.

"Why, thank you. That is much better. You must be a Maine Coon, no? You're a big fella. What's your name?"

The cat was gazing at Tobi with soulful eyes and started kneading on her abdomen.

"His name is Micky," Anna said. "We have to go now. Daddy will be really mad."

"Wait—" Tobi looked right at the cat. "Would you mind purring a little bit for my friend here?" She nodded at Troy. "He pretends he's a Big Strong Man who doesn't need anything, but I bet he'd really appreciate you."

Micky jumped down and walked over to Troy. He rubbed against Troy's legs, walking in a figure eight around him, and then looked up at Anna, who put him back in the carrier just as a new patient walked in. Anna zipped up the carrier and headed to the door.

"Remember," she turned and whispered loudly to the three of them, her index finger at her lips. "This is our secret."

CHAPTER 39

The dining area was moderately busy, with passengers eating in shifts as their appetites slowly returned. Braelyn sat down at a table with her tray of rice and dried fruit next to Devon and Amira; Troy and Tobi were sitting across the table. Amira was pushing her meal around on her plate. Her crutches were propped up next to her.

"It's so hard to figure out when it's time to eat," Devon said. "Nothing changes out here. No sunset, no sunrise…"

"Did you check out the observation deck yet?" Troy asked. "It's beyond spectacular."

"I thought all the screens went kind of gray, like there was nothing to focus on," Devon said. "I figured there wasn't much to look at. Besides," he glanced at Amira, "Amira can't get around so well."

"The gray was only in the beginning, before our brains adjusted to a new sensory input frequency. You can see stars now." Troy smiled as he spoke, but Tobi looked at Amira with concern.

"It's better you move about, Amira," Tobi said. "The more you move your leg, the more you will stimulate bone regrowth. Or maybe, are you still having some trouble with the transition to light speed?"

Amira did not look up but just shrugged, focusing intensely on moving her food from one side of the plate to the other. "I'm fine. I'm pretty tough."

Tobi frowned. "It's not about being tough. It's a psychophysiological response that we have not experienced before. Are you still feeling like your body and your mind aren't quite in sync?"

Amira looked up for the first time. "That's exactly what it feels like."

"Simon and I have been working on a treatment of sorts. It's basically a vibrating device, like a muscle massager or a TENS unit, but we've set it to vibrate at 100 Hz, which seems to be optimal at reunifying the neuromuscular pathways while recruiting comforting brain functions, like endorphin release. We've treated a few patients this way with excellent results."

"I have the Low Intensity Pulsed UltraSound unit you gave me for my leg, but to be honest, I haven't used it much," Amira said.

Tobi nodded. "You should start. But the LIPUS is high frequency, low intensity. This would be lower frequency. We used to use the transcutaneous electrical nerve stimulator, or TENS unit, set at 50 Hz for optimal stimulation of bone growth. That was before we had LIPUS. But for this... I would use the TENS unit and adjust it to 100 Hz, and instead of putting it over the fracture site, I'd want you to place it over your solar plexus and then also over the center of your forehead, between your eyes. Come see me in sick bay after lunch—or whatever we're calling this meal—and I'll give you one and show you how to regulate it."

"Chakras?" Braelyn chimed in.

"Well, yes, I guess so. It seems to be helping." Tobi turned to her meal.

"Where did you come up with that?" Braelyn asked.

Tobi and Troy exchanged a quick glance and then both shrugged in unison.

"I was just reminiscing over my beloved cats now long gone, and the healing power of their purrs," Tobi said. She turned to her meal deliberately and wouldn't meet anyone's eyes.

"Harrumph!" Braelyn said. "You met little Anna!"

Tobi nearly choked as she swallowed her lentil soup, but she said nothing more.

Russell and Kevin Burns joined them just as Tobi and Troy were leaving. Amira got up and headed out on her crutches with Devon at her side. Russell watched her go.

"Those two have become virtually inseparable," he mused. "But I'm surprised she's having so much trouble with the crutches."

"Balance in space, even when we try to match gravity, is subtly different. And maybe she's still having after effects," Kevin replied. "Warp transition or no, everything is different, and there's bound to be some who take a while to adapt."

"Yes, but *Amira*…"

"See?" Braelyn interrupted in exasperation. "That there is exactly why she can't talk to anyone about what she's feeling.

Dear brother, do you really think that just because she comes across all strong and tough that she isn't a human being inside with her own struggles? Really, Russell. Where's your compassion!"

Russell was startled. "I only meant she usually rises to any physical challenge and right now, there isn't even a threat. She can relax."

"Are you relaxed?" Braelyn demanded.

"Well, I'm trying to figure out exactly where we're headed and what we're going to do once we get there."

"And why is it always you? You were in charge of things back on Earth because the Catskills property was originally yours, but here, Captain Burns is in charge." She nodded at Kevin. "And who will be running things once we make planetfall?"

Russell was taken aback. He had no idea what to say. He just assumed he would remain the leader. "Do you think I've been unfair in the way I've run things? I got us off the planet, I kept us safe from the Whispies—"

"No," Braelyn snapped. "Angie and Arthur built this ship to get us off the planet, and Teresa made it warp-capable. Jennifer designed the Q, without which, none of this would be possible. Kevin and Shannon are piloting, with Joelle as navigator—you can't do any of that. And who knows what exactly kept us from discovery… But it doesn't matter. Everything is changed now." She stopped for a sip of iced tea, and Kevin looked uncomfortable. "We need to talk about how we are going to make decisions in our new home, Russell. You should be involved in them, but maybe not as a dictator. We had enough of that on Earth."

Russell glanced at Kevin to see his reaction, but he looked

like he'd rather be anywhere else than in the middle of an argument between the two siblings. He swallowed the rest of his stew and announced he was going back to the bridge, and left quickly.

Braelyn glared at him for a few minutes and then stormed out. Russell was left sitting by himself and was suddenly overcome with fatigue. Did everyone see him that way? As an authoritarian who needed to be in control? He thought he'd been fair and done a good job, made sure everyone was safe, and that all who wanted to come with them had the chance. He had abdicated leadership on the ship to his pilots and, of course, on the planet, formally to Erin. Was he not appreciated? He thought he had been well liked; was he wrong? But then he thought, this is my sister complaining. She's always had an obstinate side. Or was she just the only one who would dare tell him to his face what she was thinking?

Russell stared at his half-eaten lunch. He should finish it. They didn't have a lot of extra food that they could afford to waste anything, and supplies had to get them through at least another few weeks. A horrible thought came to him: Did Ganaffe think he was doing a great job just like Russell was pleased with his own performance? Was there a difference?

He ran his hands through his hair and over his face. This was ridiculous. He'd drive himself nuts this way. Just as he was about to get up, thinking he'd try out the ship's shower and see if he could wash away his muddle, a figure sat down across the table from him. He was somehow familiar, but his hair was a little grayer, and the angle of his shoulders seemed more weighted down. After a minute, Russell recognized him.

"Hello Mr. Keter."

"How's it going?" Keter answered. "Are things shaping up according to expectations?"

"I don't know what I expected, so things can't *possibly* turn out 'as expected.'"

"Your sister has a valid point. Who *should* govern the community after you find a new home?" Keter asked, staring off across the room with his brows furrowed as if he were puzzling out the answer to that question.

"I guess I really hadn't thought about it. I figured we would go on as before, to the extent possible."

"With you in charge? And that is because you have some special knowledge of foreign worlds and alien life-forms? Hmm?"

Russell said nothing.

"I told you, Mr. Vaderman. The torch has been passed."

"To my sister? Do you know how emotional she is?"

Keter turned and gazed at Russell with such an intense stare that Russell was forced to look down at his feet.

"The torch can be multifaceted. Perhaps I should say, the torch has been divided. The amazing thing about fire is that when you split it up, you do not lose intensity, you only increase the light and heat it gives off. If it has a source to burn, that is." He clasped his hands in his lap and stared at Russell.

After a moment, Keter continued. "Braelyn has already made some significant decisions without your knowledge, decisions that will have both a positive and a potentially negative effect on your new lives. But here is the point: You have been given a second chance. This is nothing less than your very last chance to escape extinction. What will you do with it? Will you continue with your old, tired way of life that you led on Earth? It's bad enough that you bring the same tired human frailties with you into the universe. Try, Mr. Vaderman, just *try* to become better people going forward. Can you do that?"

"How can I do that if I'm not in charge anymore?"

Keter shook his head in disgust. "Do you *really* think it is the ones in power who make the lasting changes? You are further gone than we thought. Frankly, we expected better from you."

Russell found himself speechless.

Keter pushed his seat back and got up. Surveying the room for a moment, he shook his head again, this time as if to himself, and walked toward the door, but he sent a parting word over his shoulder.

"Figure it out, Mr. Vaderman. And quickly."

CHAPTER 40

The crew set up the engines to initiate a secondary power burst to boost the speed of their soliton warp and this time, warned everyone that they might experience a similar reaction as before. Several TENS units had been distributed around the ship with instructions on how to use them, and there was a sense of apprehension, but their speed was increased fivefold with very little distress this time. Perhaps, as Teresa had originally suggested, their brains were no longer confounded by the effect. Still, many took advantage of the vibratory assists, and their new ETA at the Cygnus star system was now ten days away.

Of the several potential planets on which to set down, their original choice of Kepler 186f, as it had been named upon discovery, was settled upon with finality. It was the closest, and even though its sun was a red dwarf, an older, cooler star than they were accustomed to, the planet was in the Goldilocks Zone, that sweet spot just far enough from its sun to be neither too cold nor too hot. It was somewhat less dense than the Earth, meaning that the difference in gravity would take a bit of getting used to, but that should be easier than acclimating to a gravity that was stronger, making everyone feel heavier.

The time for a complete orbit around its sun was 130 days, and it was thought to have an iron and nickel core like Earth but with a higher percentage of nickel than the Earth's crust. Temperatures were estimated to average above 0°C. If there was water on the surface as predicted, and if the air had an approximate concentration of oxygen at around 20 percent, with no poisonous or severely narcosis-producing other gases, they'd call it a win. If, if, if…

There was still the problem of how they would halt the inertia of their soliton wave, which, in the near zero resistance of space, could keep the ship moving almost in perpetuity. Teresa and Kevin were working fervently with Joelle and Jennifer to plot and, on signal, automatically engage a course that would send the *Phoenix* into a sort of slingshot maneuver around Kepler 186 to slow the ship and let the star's gravity absorb most of the energy of the warp. The trick was going to be pulling out on standard power at the right moment, without being sucked into the fiery sun.

While those discussions were going on, largely on the bridge, the matter of government was slowly starting to be addressed. Anyone with interest had been invited in by lottery (there just wasn't a space aboard the *Phoenix* large enough to fit more than thirty people at a time) and some ideas were being tossed around. Russell was nervous about it. If the community felt there was no strong leadership, they might panic, and all go off on their own; Russell fully believed they were stronger together. So the objective was to explain that they were looking for members of the community to take an active role in decision making on establishing policies that would be necessary on the new world; he didn't say he might be stepping down.

There were a number of issues that would need to be addressed almost immediately. Most important was what to use as a food source, but almost as urgent was where and from what material to build shelters. It would not be good for morale to continue to live out of the ship. For that, they needed to know what to expect from the new climate. They also needed to know which plants could be harvested to be used for the necessities beyond food.

Since it was likely going to be colder than they were accustomed to, they would have to find something they could safely and inoffensively burn for warmth until they could outfit heating systems in every dwelling. The big question was how to disrupt the landscape without offending whatever natives they might find. How could they know if a plant or animal was sacred?

And then, of course, assuming there were natives, what if they proved to be hostile just because they didn't want intruders on their planet? Russell didn't even want to think how quickly a group of aliens landing on Earth would have been made unwelcome and likely killed immediately. He could only hope that the shortcomings of the human condition were not universal to sapient life everywhere.

Russell looked around the conference room. The botanist, Claire, was there, as was Angie, one of the engineers. He guessed her husband didn't draw the right straw. Joshua had shown up with his friend Monty, who was the agriculture wiz. The veterinarian, Greg, was also in attendance, as were a few people Russell didn't know well. Erika walked in as he was getting started.

"Thanks for coming in—" Russell began.

"Ain't like we got a whole lot else to do," said a man in his mid-thirties, with dark hair and bulging muscles. He was wearing a plaid flannel shirt and a baseball cap and looked like he had spent his entire life outdoors.

Russell grinned at him. "Getting a little stir-crazy? We don't have much longer to go in here. Soon we'll be on solid ground, and there will be a new set of challenges." Inwardly, Russell was hoping this was true and that they would make a safe descent and landing on a habitable planet. "It's Raymond, right? What is your area of expertise?"

"I'm a mechanic—well, I was. Mostly worked on motorcycles, but for some reason, y'all wouldn't let me bring my bike. Back on Earth, you didn't much allow us to use anything with a motor. Just horses. And me and animals, well, that's not a good match."

"Yes," Russell said, "I'm sorry. We were trying to avoid discovery."

"Right, but on this new planet, ain't no Whispies to worry about, so maybe if I can find the right materials, I can start building bikes. What'ya say?"

Russell nodded slowly. "That would be great if circumstances are favorable."

"*Now* what are you going to worry about?"

Russell hadn't realized there were such unhappy souls traveling with them and his concern grew. He was well aware that everyone had a horror story that had resulted in their fleeing what passed as civilization in America these days, but he had assumed they were grateful to have found a safe haven. And no one had been compelled to come out into space.

"Well, Raymond, first off, we don't know if the terrain will support a bike. I doubt we are going to stumble on paved roads and—"

"But that's the beauty of a motorcycle or a 'dirt bike.' We can jump right over the floor of a forest or a desert. I mean, 'slong as we got good tires and it isn't all sand that we can't get any traction from."

There was murmuring in the room.

"I am hopeful, Raymond," Russell replied. "But we'll want to first determine who else might live in the region we set down in. We may want to prove ourselves nonthreatening before we get too aggressive in overtaking the land, even in our noise production. It might be best not to draw too much attention to ourselves, in the beginning at least."

Angie spoke up. "We could probably do some modifications to dampen the sound, kind of like a muffler." She looked over at Raymond. "It won't sound as cool, to be sure, but it will make your bikes a superb asset. I imagine we are going to be spread out a bit."

"Who are you?" Raymond asked, bordering on rude.

"My name is Angie Engman. My husband and I are the engineers who designed the *Phoenix*."

That seemed to shut Raymond up pretty effectively, and Russell chuckled to himself. This was going to be interesting as each person's fears and insecurities were expressed in unique ways.

Claire raised her hand. "I'm looking forward to seeing if we can plant the grains and vegetable seeds we brought. And fruit, too, of course. If they grow, at least we know they'll be safe for us to eat and will give us our needed vitamins and nutrients."

"We want to help her," Joshua chimed in, glancing at his friend Monty. "Can we set up a botany committee? And how will we know if the plants that already grow on the new planet are safe to eat?"

"I can set up surveillance to make sure we aren't attacked without warning," Erika said. "But I feel like setting up committees isn't why you called this meeting." She looked at Russell sidelong.

"In part, it is," Russell answered. "But some of us have been talking about how we are going to make community decisions. Along with a host of advisers, I've been fulfilling that role till now, especially since I owned the land where we set up the compound. But no one owns the new planet's land, and we will be beset by a multitude of new situations, challenges, and potential dangers. Some have suggested we form some sort of governing body. Something, uh, something different from what we've experienced on Earth. Something that will hopefully be more successful."

"Sounds like we're going to need a defense unit, to be called up at a moment's notice. If the place does harbor aliens, we need to be prepared. Maybe we should suit up and scout it out to secure a site to camp," Raymond said. "I'll take shifts on that. We had some pretty potent firearms back on Earth—I hope we brought those with us!"

Russell frowned. "I'd like to reserve judgment on any alien races. *If* they exist, we have no idea whether they will be hostile or not. But they certainly will be if we threaten them.

There's bound to be a whole lot more of them than there are of us."

"Exactly!" Raymond said. "But if they see from the get-go that we can take care of ourselves, they could be more inclined to leave us alone."

Greg raised his hand from the back. "I don't disagree. Animal life across virtually all known species tends to be territorial. I mean, I don't think we should go in with guns blazing, but we need to be prepared to defend ourselves from the moment we set down."

Raymond was looking at Greg and nodding his head insolently. He glared at Russell like a challenge.

"Well," Russell said, "it will certainly be helpful if everyone finds an area where they are best suited to contribute so we can 'hit the ground running,' as the saying goes. I would like to establish that, if and when we encounter alien life, we ask questions first and shoot later. We should give it every chance to be a peaceful encounter."

"No argument there," Greg said.

"I'll post a list in the dining area of the various committees that will need to be established first. Spread the word for everyone to sign up where they think they'd be most interested and most useful. If necessary, we will shuffle people around on a temporary basis. If a person has no special skills or their skills are not immediately needed, they can be assigned to a general work force until we have basic living arrangements settled." Russell nodded at them, and the meeting broke up, leaving him feeling unsatisfied and more concerned than ever. Why did he think the question of who leads would be decided in a meeting like this? He wasn't even sure most had understood the question.

CHAPTER 41

Devon sat at the desk in his quarters, engrossed in his laptop. He couldn't quite seem to put aside the resentment he felt that despite all the incredible intellectual promise he had shown as a teenager, a "half-breed" like himself had not been permitted to go to college. His parents taught him all they could and involved him in their research, but they were both physicists, and while Devon had an aptitude for the subject, it didn't fire him up like music and mathematics did as they related to communication. His intuition assured him that sentient beings had a common basic language and that music could be employed to express universal ideas. That was, if the emotions that music evoked in humans were ubiquitous across species somehow, but, of course, there was no guarantee of that. To that end, he had acquired and mastered the flute, as it was a versatile instrument he could carry around in his pocket.

The *Phoenix* had brought a wealth of information out into

space with the aid of the Q as well as multiple traditional computer systems for general passenger access. The annals of every subject that had ever been studied and recorded for as far back as human history was known to go were available to them. Under the rule of Ganaffe, most knowledge had become taboo, yet scholars had managed to secretly preserve much of humanity's treasures. But accessing those archives was still not nearly the same as studying with peers, people he could bounce ideas off. Devon could not shed the taste of bitterness from how cruelly he had been treated, to have so much ability and denied opportunity, simply because his father was of dark skin. There were times when his anger threatened to fill him up.

His mother was also a bit of a hybrid, part American Indian and part African American, but her mother had been pure Caucasian, and her skin tone belied her roots unless one looked very carefully. It was mainly the coarse, black curly hair that gave anyone reason to question.

There was a quiet knock on the door, and Devon immediately put aside his equations. Hoping to see Amira, he jumped up and ran his hand through his hair like a comb in a futile attempt to straighten it. "Come in!"

It took a few minutes for Devon to recognize the man who greeted him. It was the stranger who had helped bring him into the compound after he had collapsed in the forest.

"Sa-Sahina?"

"Yes." Sahina gave him a warm smile. "May I come in and visit with you?" Sahina did not wait for an answer; as polite as his words were, they weren't really a request. He wandered purposefully over to the computer so that Devon wished he had minimized the work he'd been doing.

"You are very gifted, young man," Sahina said; it was almost as if he understood at a glance what Devon had been working on. "You know, you don't need to be at a university to make startling and important discoveries. Back in the earlier days of mankind, major breakthroughs were made far outside of formal institutions of learning. Think of the first lightbulb. Or automobile...or airplane. The telephone, for example." He looked at Devon with an intensity that made Devon uncomfortable. "Believe in yourself. You have a true gift."

Devon felt the blood rush to his cheeks. *Who was this guy?* But it was nice to hear someone acknowledge him. His mother was way too busy to notice what he was up to, especially lately—not that he blamed her. Dad was the one who had always encouraged and coached him, and Dad was gone now. Forever.

Devon immediately smashed his feelings below the surface. He still wasn't ready to deal with that. The anger, the grief, the loss...the guilt. He swallowed hard.

"There's something strange about you," Devon said to Sahina. "I don't mean any disrespect, but I don't understand you. Where did you come from that day? Why are you so secretive? I can't tell if you want to be here with us or not. I'm sorry, I don't mean to offend—"

Sahina chuckled. "You are very perceptive, Devon, and no, I take no offense. I don't *feel* any offense in your intention. You can feel these things, too, can't you? Don't let them frighten you. It will only make you a better, more skilled communicator."

Devon almost didn't realize how Sahina had evaded his question. Almost. Now he was getting suspicious.

"I *feel* like you were not lost when we met you. I feel like you knew exactly where you were, and you wanted us to stumble upon you and have it look like an accident. But I don't know why."

Sahina nodded and turned aside. He sat down in one of the chairs that were bolted into the floor and motioned for Devon to take a seat opposite.

"I'm sorry about your father," Sahina said, as if he knew what Devon had been pondering a moment ago. "And yes, you are correct. I won't deflect you again; you're too smart and you deserve better from me. Please accept that I just cannot share that with you right now. I can only tell you that you are right, and you will understand soon. After we make planetfall."

"So you think it will work? My mom's equations, the strategy to slingshot around the sun… and we will land on a habitable planet?"

Sahina cocked his head sidewise. "You think I have some special insight? Some… precognition of events as they will play out?"

"Yes," Devon said. "I do."

"Hmm," was Sahina's response, and he raised his eyebrows as if he had never considered this. After a moment, he got up to leave. "It's been nice chatting with you, Devon." And abruptly, he walked out.

Devon was more confused than ever. He turned back to his computer program, wondering what in the world—any world—that was all about just as Amira came to the door and tapped it gently with one of her crutches.

"Hi!" Devon couldn't conceal his happiness to see her. "How are you feeling? How's your leg?"

"Unsettling," Amira answered. She came in and sat on one of the beds to put her leg up. "I've had broken bones before, but this is just...it feels weird. Dr. Lister says it's because of the artificial gravity, and she gave me a whole dissertation about how our bones replace themselves every day by responding to the stress of gravity and movement. She took x-rays and said it was progressing along as expected—whatever that means." Amira shrugged. "I'm sure she knows what she's talking about, but I got the feeling there was something she wasn't telling me. It's been two and a half weeks, and she had said it was an ancillary bone, so I'd have thought it would be feeling better."

"Can you put any weight on it at all?"

"Yeah, I mean, I can walk on it with a limp, but I could do that from the beginning, once the wound was closed. I'm afraid I won't be as fast as I was, and if we make a successful landing and find a place to colonize, I *need* to know I'll be quick on my feet and able to respond to whatever we encounter. I'm troubled."

"But Dr. Lister thinks you will be fine?"

"Dr. Lister didn't really say. But she holds things close to her chest, that one. All with good intentions, I think." Amira laughed.

They sat in a comfortable silence for a few minutes. "How's your program coming along?" Amira asked.

Devon brightened up immediately. "Not bad. If we encounter another species with hearing similar to our own, I think I can reach out to them in a nonthreatening way with music. And I'm quantifying notes into a language of sorts, something we already understand but typically don't verbalize."

"Do the captain and Russell know what you've accomplished?"

It was Devon's turn to shrug. "I don't think so. My mother knows what I've been working on but not how far I've gotten. Who's going to be in charge of everything once we land? That's the person I should talk to."

"I don't know. I'm not really sure of anything anymore," Amira said.

———

Russell found Teresa gazing at the stars on the observation deck. Her hands were planted flat on the sill in front of the great window, and she looked like she was straining to see beyond the farthest stars. Russell walked up to stand nearly shoulder to shoulder with her. She barely moved, as if she knew he was there, and his presence did not surprise her in the least.

"Where is your head right now?" Russell asked her.

Teresa glanced at him briefly and then turned back to the window. "Thinking of my husband. We both worked so hard for this, and for him to die when we were this close... The universe had a harsh plan for us." She looked down at a blue pencil she was holding and started spinning it between her fingers.

"I'm sorry," Russell said.

Teresa shook her head. "Richard would say that he had finished doing what he was put on the Earth to do, that he was no longer needed in the world, whereas Devon and I apparently still have work to do in the outer reaches. But... I wish I could share this with him. I wish he could see these stars. I wish he could sense the enormity of space… He would have loved this."

"Perhaps he is watching," Russell said. "He is part of the vastness of the universe now." Russell started to put his hand over hers, then thought better of it and took it back. "How did you two meet?"

Teresa turned toward him and smiled. "We met at MIT in 2001. He was a senior and I was a sophomore. You know, back then, we thought that 9/11 was the worst thing our country would ever have to go through. We were in New York City together the very weekend before the attack; we had dinner at the top of the World Trade Center and spent the afternoon in Battery Park. I mean, we were *right there.* We literally dodged the bullet by seven days. It was one of the moments that really bonded us, I think. Richard was not only the most brilliant man I ever met, but also the most poised and calm. Always looking for the appropriate response but willing to accept fate as it happened, regardless of its consequences. He was a pure, enlightened genius."

"I wish I could have met him."

"Yes, you would have liked each other. Quite a lot, I imagine," Teresa said. "Well, I'm off to sleep now. Enjoy the view. For all we know, it could be our last."

CHAPTER 42

The moment had come. The *Phoenix* was approaching the Kepler 186 star system and would be past it in less than two hours if they did not find a way to stop. If initiating a warp soliton was brand new science, putting the brakes on was even more uncertain.

The knowledge of how to move at faster-than-light speed had been around for decades, but the *Phoenix* was the first to accomplish it in fact. Stopping the process with specific coordinates in mind had only just been postulated, and the calculations could not be made until they were close enough to Kepler 186 to get an exact assessment of its specific mass and gravity.

The red dwarf was much older than Earth's Sol and with less abundance of heavy metals, but there was one planet within the habitable zone. The idea was to shut down the warp just as they were passing closely by the star and let its gravity pull the ship toward it with enough traction to slow them down. Then they would have to quickly initiate conventional thrusters to pull themselves out of the sun's gravity, leaving the *Phoenix* solidly within the star system under autonomous control. From there, they could plot a course for the planet, Kepler 186f.

There was a major concern that the psychoneurological debilitating effect of going into warp speed might again affect them as they came out of it, leaving them hurtling toward the sun without anyone consciously flying the ship. They had not anticipated this being a problem when they set out, as they had yet to experience the severe disorientation of the change in speed. Or rather, the change in their very substance.

Anything traveling faster than light essentially ceased to be matter and was converted to pure energy. Minds naturally operated as pure energy, but under normal conditions, they experienced themselves as connected to physical bodies. At warp speed, both mind and body were essentially discorporate, unsubstantial; neither existed on the material plane at all. Now their bodies were going to be transmuted back so that their consciousnesses again engaged with their physical forms, while their minds should presumably remain as energy webs. The effects were an unknown, so what they might need to do to compensate was not predictable.

As soon as they had exact measurements of the star Kepler 186, Jennifer worked feverishly with Kevin and Joelle, inputting expected gravitational forces into the Q and projecting course calculations to pull them out of the gravitational field precisely when needed so that even if no one was flying the ship, the autopilot would do what had to be done.

Of course, they had always intended for Q to make the rapid calculations and changes exponentially faster than mere humans could, but not knowing if they would have eyes on the action was unnerving.

The passengers were all strapped down in their respective seats in their living quarters and on the bridge. Braelyn was up top with them in case there was an immediate need for her to reach out psychically to some new life form. Kevin looked at Russell as if waiting for a signal. It was still habit to defer to Russell, but he was starting to grow into his role. He had no idea what his function was going to be once they made landfall—*if* they made landfall.

"Attention, everyone. This is Captain Burns. We are preparing to disintegrate the warp. Please make sure you are all fastened into your places. We all remember how disorienting it was when we entered this state; we do not know how it will feel to leave it. When we accelerated to the speed of light, there was no sensation of movement; slowing down into normal space-time may be quite different. We may be tossed around a bit. That's why it's very important that you stay strapped in." He cut the comm and looked around the bridge at each person, measuring their readiness for what they were about to do, and perhaps looking for a shot of courage. He opened the comm again.

"We are going to be relying on this new sun for our successful entrance into its solar system. This sun was named Kepler 186." He paused. "But we will refer to it now as just Kepler. May God be with us."

He turned off the communication and nodded to his navigator. Joelle cut the soliton generator while aiming the *Phoenix* directly at Kepler, and Jennifer reached up and stroked the Q as if encouraging a devoted pet.

At first, they felt nothing. Then pressure. In their ears, in their heads, it was like they were suddenly thirty feet under-water. There was a sensation of slowing down, but it was in their heads, not their bodies. Several of them squeezed their eyes shut tightly, and this time Erika did vomit, all over her lap. But no one lost consciousness.

Kevin was gripping his controls as if he might be thrown across the room, but his eyes were wide open. He was the only one who had trained in acceleration changes before this journey, and he was determined to stay focused. He gritted his teeth.

It was like moving in slow motion compared to what they had been looking at before. Kepler appeared on the front screen, getting larger by the second.

"We're going to crash—we're getting sucked in!" Braelyn screamed. "We're too close!"

Joelle shouted back, even though it was quiet on the bridge. "We are about 67.5 million miles away. About the distance from Venus to our Sol. We have to get *much* closer."

Everything was silent yet it felt like there was a high intensity, high frequency whine. It was, again, hard to think. The mental discipline of Kevin, Joelle, and Jennifer was outstanding, as they maintained monitoring even as Devon and Teresa became semiconscious. Russell struggled visibly.

Seconds ticked by, and the red sun grew in size on the screen. It was dimmer than Sol but fiery and ominous. The screen's filters made it possible to gaze at it without burning out their retinae. It was terrifying.

When the red ball of fire completely filled the screen, Jennifer called out. "Now! Q should be initiating course alter-ation, now!"

Sure enough, the *Phoenix* began to turn slightly. It felt like the movie *Titanic* when the ship starts turning and everyone wonders if it will miss the iceberg. Which, of course, it did not.

Kevin's hands were pulling on a lever at his console until his knuckles were white, as if he was making the turn himself. Years of flying fighter jets were a habit he couldn't break at the moment. The whole process only took seconds but felt like an eternity. The fireball ultimately moved alongside them and grew even larger, if that were possible, but they no longer seemed to be heading straight into it. They could feel the pull on the *Phoenix*, and they all wondered if she might break apart as she bucked the star's gravity.

As they continued around the sun, the ship seemed to move more slowly and finally, the fiery globe was passing ever so subtly to the rear. They held their breaths like that for another thirty seconds until it was clear that they really were passing the sun.

"All engines, forward thrust," Kevin barked. There was another sensation of tug-of-war that lasted about thirty seconds and then a sudden release, and the *Phoenix* was moving forward on its own. Kevin was sweating.

They cruised like that for another ten minutes until the sun was only visible on the rear screens. "Cut to half power," he said softly. "I think we did it." Shoulders slumped in relief all around the room, and the crew on the bridge erupted in whoops of excitement.

"Captain Burns!" The intercom crackled.

"Yes?"

"It's Jeremy in the engine room. The cooling system is failing. We're too damn hot!"

CHAPTER 43

Kevin and Teresa ran for the engine room with Russell in tow, and Arthur Engman arrived just as they did. The temperature in the room was easily over 100°F, and the blast of hot air hit them in the face as they walked in. Jeremy was running from station to station with sweat streaming down his face, and when he saw them, he waved them over frantically. "Don't touch anything, I already made that mistake," he said, and held up his right hand to show them an angry blister on his palm.

Russell had expected the problem to be with the warp core, but it was the conventional engines that were emitting an ominous, low-pitched hum.

"These engines were never designed to pull away from a force as strong as a sun from such a close distance," Jeremy said.

"Let's just shut it down entirely. Shannon can make sure

we drift between planets until they can be restarted," Kevin said and was about to give the order.

"Wait," Arthur interjected. "If we shut them down completely, we might have a hard time revving them up again. Pull them down to minimum power, with just a small current of energy flowing through them. Let's see what we can do to cool them off. We need to navigate to our final destination, and we'll need them to finely control our landing course and velocity as we go through the planet's atmosphere."

"What are going to cool them with?" Russell asked. "We don't have enough water to spare, and it's not going to be of sufficient temperature—"

"Water will do nothing for this," Teresa said.

Arthur was alternately nodding and shaking his head. "We don't have anything to cool this puppy off."

"Friends," Teresa grinned. "We are surrounded by an *immense* cooling source."

They all turned to her, perplexed.

"Space, gentlemen. We are in deep space. It is *very* cold out there."

"Well, that's creative," Arthur muttered. "But how do you suggest we bring the cold *in here*?"

Teresa frowned. "I haven't quite worked that part out yet. But if we could somehow decrease the insulation of the hull in this room only…"

"Yes!" Arthur said. "There is a narrow passageway between the hull and the ship proper throughout the length of the *Phoenix*, for accessing equipment. And we have airlocks spread around the ship as well. We could suit up and open a few airlocks, let the temperature drop, and…it could work!"

"Would the temperature change be localized only in the engine room?" Russell asked.

"Well, no," Arthur said, "but we can use the airlocks closest to this area. The whole ship will start to get pretty cold if we leave them open long enough, but it should be most pronounced closest to the opened regions. We should minimize energy use right now anyway. I'd reduce the ambient temperature to 40°F while we open the door. Hopefully the system will cool down quickly."

That wasn't going to go over big with the passengers, who deserved an explanation and an update on what had transpired since they broke out of faster-than-light speed, but there was no time for that. The engines were suffering heat damage with every second they stayed at these temperatures.

Kevin spoke to Shannon who made an announcement to everyone that they had succeeded in arriving at their destination solar system, and they could unstrap from their seats and move about. She also stated, as matter-of-factly as she could, that it was going to get cold for a spell and everyone should find and don their warm jackets. She assured them there was no danger and asked for them to hold their questions for the time being and a full assessment of their progress so far would be provided shortly.

Two crewmen, James Foster and Renée Williams, went to the closest airlock station and put on space suits. Then they tethered themselves and entered into the corridor that ran between the ship proper and deep space outside. Opening the outside airlocks brought with it zero gravity, but these two had trained for this, if only in their imaginations.

The engine temperature was registering around 310°C, which was getting dangerously close to the temperature at which the diamond film covering some of the components would melt. While the structural metals had higher melting points, not all of the engine was built with metal, and there was a danger that there could be fusion of internal parts.

Once the airlocks were open, there was not much to do but wait. The ventilation system was set at maximum, and they all left the engine room, except for Jeremy, now in his own space suit, and tethered to a wall with a thick cord. They also opened the airlock which allowed ejection of matter from the engine room in case an emergency evacuation of an overloaded component became necessary, and watched the temperature gauges.

Throughout the ship, there was a lot of complaining and questioning, as passengers shivered unless they were in their insulated parkas, and Shannon did her best to keep everyone calm, using her title as Captain Giveners, and struggling to sound authoritative and composed.

The engine room itself cooled down quickly, but the massive thruster engines slowly crept down the temperature scale. It took several hours, but the alerts went off and the outside of the consoles became warm but no longer hot enough to burn a hand. They swapped out shifts of astronauts manning the open airlocks as well as the engine room, so there was no risk of anyone running out of oxygen or spending too much time in zero gravity.

At four hours, Shannon radioed down that they were going to need some impulse power to navigate around one of the planets. The last thing they wanted was to stretch the engines by letting them enter the gravitational field of a planet that was unlikely to be life sustaining.

They increased power gently, giving the *Phoenix* just

enough energy to make a wide berth around the orb. Anyone on the observation deck could get a spectacular view of it, and Braelyn and Joshua were not missing out. Slowly, they passed a great purple and brown gaseous ball with rings of yellow and orange cloudlike vapors surrounding it. There were a few telescopes positioned on the decks for people to take turns gazing through, and they were being made good use of.

"Is that what Jupiter looked like up close?" Joshua asked.

"No clue," Braelyn said, but she was awestruck by the sight, as were many passengers who had come up to look around.

Caleb stood there with his father, Greg, and whispered, "It was all worth it, Dad. Even if we die out here, just to *see* this, what no one else has ever seen."

Greg looked down at his son as if he were seeing him for the first time. Sure, Caleb had been forced to leave his childhood behind at a bitterly young age, but the statement, coming from an eleven-year-old, gave him the chills. Especially when it was his own eleven-year-old.

"I don't think we're going to die, Caleb—"

"Yeah, but, Dad, why did it get so cold, and so...quiet? I think the engines are off. I didn't notice the sound until it went away. And they told us to get our warm gear. I wish Alana were here to see this..."

Greg put his arm around his son's shoulder. "Let's hope not, Cay. And, yeah, I miss her too."

The other advantage of hovering in the solar system, other than experiencing the majesty of outer space up close and in slow motion, was that the Q was able to take accurate measurements of conditions on all the orbiting planets.

The planets closer to the sun, like the one seen at the observation deck, were hot and gaseous and not possibilities for settlement. The first four planets were also tidally locked or near so, meaning that the length of a day could be thirty to fifty times as long as a day on Earth was. But the fifth planet from the sun, Kepler 186f, was in the Goldilocks Zone and seemed to have an atmosphere comprised of a mixture of nitrogen, oxygen, and argon, like Earth. There was a tenth of a percent more helium than on Earth, but they could get used to that. Carbon dioxide levels were barely perceptible, so either there were no life forms exhaling the gas or the local flora was processing it efficiently, much the way Earth used to function—before levels reached the current 0.45 percent that bordered on toxicity to human life. The surface temperature was currently about 8°C, or 46°F, and miraculously, the planet also appeared to be largely blue, presaging water over a high percentage of the surface. They might have found a new home—if they could only get there and land safely.

CHAPTER 44

t took thirty-six hours for the engine temperatures to completely return to normal. They had closed the airlocks after five hours and raised the ambient temperature aboard the *Phoenix* to 50°F long before and then just waited it out, asking for as little functioning from the massive system as possible. There was a lot of time for the travelers to stargaze, settle into groups who wanted to establish homes near each other, and speculate about what they might find on Kepler 186f. Now that they could actually see their destination, the mood was cautiously joyful.

Several families committed to remaining close to each other and there was a growing desire for community to enhance a feeling of security. There was no doubt the miniature society would be close knit.

Braelyn met with Joshua and Russell for a bite to eat before they started the engines back up to normal cruising speed. It was the first that they had gotten together as a family in months, even before the unhappy rush to leave the Earth behind. Joshua was chattering on about how beautiful space was and how gazing at the planets made it feel like they were all in a science fiction movie. It was almost as if he had reverted to his younger years, when he had been charmingly immature for his age, slightly on the spectrum of being intellectually challenged, and excited about everything. Had their shift in space-time somehow altered his brain chemistry back to the way he was before he had been dosed with scopolamine?

Fourteen years ago, Russell's wife had enrolled Joshua in a government sponsored learning program called Cingulate Services. Unbeknownst to any of them, it relied on feeding small doses of scopolamine to the clients. This allowed for the suggestion that they were capable of functioning in a smarter and more capable way than they had so far achieved, and the compulsory properties of the drug made it very successful. The students did not know why they were getting smarter, they just found themselves more adept at everything. If it hadn't been used for such nefarious purposes, it would have been an amazing tool. But it was also a first step in mind control; the drug made it impossible for a person to disobey a command and left them amnestic to the entire incident.

Joshua had befriended someone in his group who was being used by the government to test the limits of scopolamine control. Quite by accident, Joshua ended up smack in the middle of a murder scene of which he later had no recollection—except that he woke up covered in someone else's blood. The event thrust Russell into an investigation of what happened to his nephew and led him to discover that he, himself, was somehow immune to scopolamine—and more

—he could reverse its effect on Joshua. Russell then became a person of interest to the facets of authority who were looking to control the entire population. This, in turn, led him back to his experience in the Northern Peruvian Andes at the age of three, when the shaman had summoned him to the smoke-filled hut, and Russell had become intoxicated with Devil's Breath and a variety of other hallucinogens, causing a mutation in his brain chemistry. It all seemed like forever ago now.

Joshua continued to chat away enthusiastically, just as he had before attending the Cingulate Services group until finally, Braelyn had had enough.

"Hush, Josh. There is a lot to talk about that needs to be settled."

Joshua looked like he'd been slapped. Braelyn had become so much more patient with her son as her own mental faculties had matured; now she was slipping back into psychological habits she had not displayed for nearly a decade. Russell frowned.

"Do you two feel any different after the transition to and from warp speed?" Russell asked.

"Different how? Like, in the head?" Braelyn asked. "You mean, because I feel a little short tempered? Seriously, Russell. We've been in space for a month now, I think I have the right to be impatient! When are we going to land on this new planet, anyway? It's time we got off this ship and smelled some fresh air."

Russell chuckled.

"What?" Braelyn demanded.

"Well, we have no idea what 'fresh air' will smell like on this new planet. If there's a lot of sulfur in the atmosphere, it might smell like rotten eggs," Russell said, and Joshua cracked up laughing.

"That's hardly funny!" Braelyn said. "I think I would shoot myself."

Russell looked at her with concern. His sister *had* once been suicidal but not since she had learned to control her mind. He changed the subject.

"Following up on your earlier worry, we have not made any decisions about how we will govern ourselves. What rules we should establish, who decides those rules, what we should do about anyone who violates them. I think we should set a precedent before we land. What do you think?"

"I think you're still trying to be a dictator," Braelyn said. "No one owns this new world, and no one is entitled to set up laws of behavior. I think we will all get along just fine without government. Haven't we had enough of that? For God's sake, Russ. What's with you and the power trip?"

Russell felt like he'd been sucker punched. "I just thought...to keep each other safe. We are stronger together. There are a lot of potential dangers. We know nothing about this planet and the people who may be living here."

"*Potential* dangers, *may* be people living there...geez, let's see what the place is like first," Braelyn said. "Maybe we can all just be good neighbors. There aren't *that* many of us, after all, and we all know each other."

Russell bit his lip. Was Braelyn right? "But, Brae, in order for us to survive here over time, we will have to increase our numbers."

Braelyn snorted. "Let's first see if we like it enough to survive here."

Joshua was looking back and forth from the mother who

had basically abandoned him as a child to the uncle who had raised him. Discord between them had been the norm when he was young, but it had not been in front of him for a long time. Now he was thirty-six years old but was somehow being transported back to those years.

Sahina Keter appeared suddenly at their table and helped himself to a seat. The conversation abruptly stopped as the family stared at the visitor. He looked at each one in turn for a long moment, his piercing eyes seeming to fillet them open and scrutinize their souls.

Finally, he nodded and broke the silence. "You will do better here," he said. It was not a question, not really even a statement of fact. It was a command.

"You must not repeat the mistakes of the past."

"But starting out with a few people telling everyone else what to do is exactly the same as what we had back on Earth!" Braelyn said.

Russell was shaking his head. "I hardly think anarchy is the right option. We have to have some sort of central leadership for protection and for equitable distribution of resources," he said.

"That's only if resources are scarce and if there is imminent danger!" Braelyn shouted back.

"Children." They both looked at Keter in surprise. At fifty-six and sixty years old, they did not expect anyone to call them "children." Only Joshua grinned at the reprimand.

Keter shook his head sadly. "Why can't you see? You are being given an opportunity to start over. We want you to succeed," he said.

"Who's 'we'?" Russell and Braelyn asked at the same time.

Joshua asked, "How do we do that?"

Sahina turned to Joshua and his gaze was gentle. "By changing what is in your hearts. By changing your attitudes. By changing the perspective with which you view the universe and all the worlds and life existing in it."

He smiled at Joshua, the first genuine sign of affection any of them had ever seen from Sahina. "Any form of government can work well. No government at all can also work well. As long as you are *all* united in your respect and goodwill toward each other and toward any and every living thing, every *single* piece of creation. That is all you need. And it is imperative that you each find it within yourselves."

CHAPTER 45

"Everyone should be strapped into your seats. We are preparing to enter the atmosphere of Kepler 186f," Captain Kevin Burns's voice sounded through the ship's comms.

"This planet appears to be habitable. We will take further measurements of the atmosphere when we land before we open the doors as well as scan for other life forms. It's been a very long trip and I know you are all restless, but please be patient just a little bit longer. When we do embark from the *Phoenix*, please remember: We are the intruders. Be respectful of everything that exists here. We have no way of knowing what might be sacred to some other culture. And stay in groups. I don't want anyone getting lost or finding themselves vulnerable to the environment—or anything else. Okay, here we go."

The vision from the bridge screens was breathtaking.

Swirling white clouds over a planet that was half blue and half a mixture of green and deep reddish brown.

"Ready to engage heat shields," Shannon reported, "but we are going to orbit at fifteen kilometers, or almost fifty thousand feet, and look around for an appropriate landing area, which keeps us out of the lower atmosphere for now, but allows us to get a good look at the planet surface. Hey! There appears to be *ice* on the poles!"

They all cheered. Ice meant water. Water meant potential for plant and animal life to thrive.

Shannon adjusted course to be at the equator, where it was bound to be warmer. Jennifer was taking readings from the Q.

"Looks like the ambient temperature is around 5°C, or 40°F at the equator; this area represents late spring. We're not likely to have any summer temperatures in the nineties, like we had on Earth," Jennifer said.

Devon was in his place by the communication console, looking like he felt superfluous. "Does that mean our crops won't grow? We brought along a lot of seeds, didn't we?"

"Hopefully the vegetation that grows here will be edible and tasty. It's better not to introduce new species anyway. We don't know what our crops might do to the ecosystem that exists here," Russell said.

They descended slowly, watching the forward screen that showed them both the air in front of them and they also had a magnified thumbnail picture of what the land directly below looked like. Something plantlike was down there, covering the ground completely, so they could not see beneath it.

"I've located an area of flat land, about a hundred meters long by thirty meters wide. It's deep red and somewhat luminous. We can land there, it seems otherwise deserted," Joelle said.

"Initiating landing sequence," Kevin said.

They all held their breaths.

The *Phoenix* was an immense ship, but the area Joelle had identified seemed to be tailor made for them, like a personal landing strip. The *Phoenix* went into hover mode, floating slowly down to the ground. The landing gear came out and they set down as gently as a feather coming to rest.

Joelle looked to the captains for further instruction. Just as Kevin was about to direct her to turn off the engines, they felt even more than heard a rumbling below them, and the *Phoenix* shook on ground that suddenly seemed to give way.

"Lift off!" Kevin shouted. The engines reversed, and the *Phoenix* fought the gravity of the planet, which seemed to be opening up beneath them. The ship pitched to the side, and they all grabbed their seats as Shannon and Kevin pulled on the controls to lift them back up. There was a scraping sound and vibration against the starboard hull as they rose to a few hundred meters and looked below, where a great hole in the planet surface revealed itself, steaming from pockets of moisture.

"What the hell is that?" Joelle asked.

"Sinkhole of some sort," Jennifer answered. She was hanging on to the bar that surrounded the Q. "I don't know why we didn't detect it before landing. The density read as solid."

"Is the whole surface going to be like that?" Shannon asked.

"Perhaps the equator is not the best place to land," Jennifer said. "Let's move north. It will be colder but perhaps the ground will be harder. I am reprogramming the Q to recognize that type of surface in the future."

"What was the ground made of?" Kevin asked.

"Some sort of solid gas, if that makes sense. The pressure of our weight broke it open. If we had shut down engines, there would not have been time to restart before we were sucked into the planet. The temperatures just below the surface are a lot hotter than they should be. It's weird, to be sure. Q has never seen anything like it before."

They cruised for a half hour, just looking down at the surface, wondering what other surprises this planet might be holding in store for them.

They passed over a region that looked like it had huts of some kind built on it. Heartened by the prospect of a more solid ground but wary of what their interaction with a new species might bring, they cruised for another thousand miles before setting down at the same longitude. They left the engines on for a solid ten minutes and had the Q run multiple sensory scans.

The ground beneath was made up of nickel and iron, more nickel than iron, but the iron was closer to the surface, giving the ground a reddish hue. It seemed solid down to fifty meters. There was apparently some sort of energy field that was interfering with their scanners, but as far as they could tell, it did not look like it would be better anywhere else on the planet.

They scanned the air composition and confirmed an oxygen, nitrogen atmosphere, similar to that of the Earth. The slightly more helium and argon concentrations might have a narcotic effect on some supersensitive people, but for most of them, it should still be okay. Then they searched around the

Phoenix for heat signals that might indicate mobile life forces and found none, at least not for a ten-mile radius.

Kevin ordered the engines shut down and unstrapped himself from his command console. "Well, let's see where we are!"

A small group of them assembled at the main airlock. They were wearing warm parkas, gloves, and hats, as the temperature outside registered at 3°C. Russell, Kevin Burns, Devon Simmons, and the two crew members who had donned the space suits to cool down the *Phoenix* disembarked together. All but Devon were carrying sidearms, but they were slung from their shoulders, and not being held at the ready, as there were no readings of life forms close by.

Devon looked around cautiously as they walked outside. There was some sort of red vegetation growing in patches about five inches tall. There was a slight breeze and the air smelled fresh—but unfamiliar. It was not unpleasant, but it definitely did not smell like air back home. As he took a few steps, he seemed like he might fly off into the air.

"The gravity is less than that of Earth's, so you will feel lighter and more agile," Kevin said. "Be careful that you don't go running off faster than you intended, you'll be out of control. It will just take some getting used to."

The sun was starting to set, and as it did, a chill wind whipped up, biting through their warm clothes. The sky was a mixture of red, purple, and orange, and streaks of pale white clouds stretched across the sky all the way to the horizon.

They each looked around in the immediate vicinity. They'd have to wait until morning to do any serious exploring and were hopeful that even with a red sun, there'd be a lot more ambient light. James and Renée were scanning for any obvious hazards, but it was clear that their first excursion beyond the immediate vicinity of the ship should be done in daylight.

Devon wandered carefully over to some rocks at the periphery of the clearing and squatted down to examine them. There were some markings or runes on them, obviously placed in a deliberate order. He ran his finger over the grooves and traced the carvings, which were inset about half a centimeter from the surface. Language? His breath quickened.

"Hey, over here!" Devon called out.

Kevin came quickly and stooped to have a look. He turned a flashlight on the stones and looked at Devon with amazement and then turned back to the tablets. There were only three of them that were marked, and those were clustered together. Several others of similar shape were scattered around and were smooth.

At that moment, Russell called to everyone to return to the ship. The temperature had dropped precipitously, and the darkness came abruptly and was nearly complete. As they made their way reluctantly back inside, Renée pointed at the sky. "Look!"

A moon was just rising on the horizon. Its color was dull fuchsia, which might have been reflecting the setting sun or might have been due to some unknown elements in its crust. It stood out in contrast to the sky, which was now a dark purple.

"How beautiful…" Renée's voice trailed off.

The next day, virtually all the travelers came out to breathe the air and look at their new home, an alien world. In daylight, the tablets from the night before looked even more like symbols of a civilization. Several parties went out to explore, but no structures or signs of any technology were visible. There was a forest of unfamiliar trees to the east and a rock quarry about a mile away. Ample resources to build houses, but the knowledge that *someone* had been there and left their mark made it unnerving to consider setting down roots there.

The weary travelers picnicked outside and slept in the ship for a few days, waiting to see if anyone would show. They posted guards who were prepped to use firearms only in cases of dire danger, but the place seemed utterly deserted.

Scouting parties went out daily and consistently reported back a countryside of reddish-green trees and shrubbery, flowers of pink and purple and a few orange, and no sign of danger. Berries grew on some of the bushes, but they had yet to determine if they were safe to eat. They had landed on an area of plains, and there were ample clear, flat regions to walk on. The dirt under their feet was tan and rust colored and flat enough to drive a sedan over, but there were no paved roads anywhere, and no tire tracks they could find. A few miles away, they had found another cluster of stones with runes carved into three of them, set off in a semicircle, but no other signs of civilization were uncovered. Claire had gone along on some of the scouting parties to explore the local vegeta-tion, and she likened the runes to road signs, but to where they led was anyone's guess. So far, it was the only hint of intelligent life.

Finally, they decided to set up a more solid camp. They chose to use rocks for structure and to cover them with wood and thatch from trees in the Red Forest, as they started calling it. It felt good to actually be doing something. After two weeks, still no creature approached them, but Braelyn said her neck prickled frequently, and she was sure they were being watched.

Amira's leg had not healed as well as hoped. She could walk without crutches, but there was a definite limp, and anyone paying attention could see that every step was mildly painful. Tobi had been unable to x-ray her once they landed. The energy field that had interfered with their scanners seemed to be disrupting a lot of their equipment. It was not even a certainty that they could get the *Phoenix* to lift off again if they wanted to. The systems were being more destabilized the longer they stayed on the planet surface.

But the mood soon gave way to relief and even joy, as everyone chipped in to help each other build homes for themselves and their families, and what would soon become akin to extended families. A stream of fresh tasting, potable water was discovered at the edge of the Red Forest and some small creatures were noted hiding among the short bushes nearby. As of yet, none of them came close, and Braelyn kept the wolves from hunting them—although she wasn't sure how long she could continue that. They were pretty restless from their trip as well.

The scenery was spectacular, the skies were crystal clear, and there were two moons that graced them every night. It frequently rained in the hours just before dawn, causing new flowers to bloom every day. It was easily one of the most beautiful places any of them could have imagined.

Micky the Maine Coon was seen prowling the forest at times, particularly at night, but if he had disturbed anything, it wasn't obvious, and Anna, who had prided herself on being Micky's "confidant," was not able to tell where he'd been or what he had found. He was most frequently in the company of little Anna because she cried when he left her, but he had an attitude of superiority about him, as if he knew much about their new planet that the little colony did not. But maybe that was just consistent with his being a cat.

EPILOGUE

Two months after they made planetfall, a group of the earthlings stood outside several completed dwellings following a brief rain shower, admiring their handiwork and the beauty of the rich landscape. They were getting used to the foliage being green with a reddish hue, and there were purple rolling hills way off to the north that they could see when the skies were clearest. Greg was behind the nearest house examining tracks in the wet ground and making observations about what sort of creature would have left them, and Teresa stood nearby with Russell, taking deep breaths. Two hundred yards away, Monty was walking through a newly planted field of indigenous grain that tasted somewhat like spelt.

"I feel like every breath I take makes me more at peace in this place. It's claiming us. Do you feel it?" Teresa asked.

Russell looked alarmed, but Devon appeared at her side

and took an exaggerated breath of his own. "I do," Devon said. "I *think* it's a good thing."

A crow-like bird flew to the top of the newly constructed home and cawed loudly as Sahina Keter casually strolled up to them. He seemed to have appeared out of nowhere.

"Hi!" Devon said. "Where have you been?"

"Out and about, like yourselves."

"There is an indigenous people living here," Russell said.

"Well, of course," Sahina said. "You didn't think a beautiful place like this was for you alone, did you?"

"How come we haven't seen them?" Teresa asked.

Sahina looked into her eyes the way he had when they'd first met in the hallway of the complex back on Earth, what seemed like eons ago. "They are deciding what to do about you, I would guess. That is what I would be doing."

"You've met them, haven't you? You've talked to them!" Devon was animated and more direct than the others would have dared, yet somehow it didn't sound offensive coming from him.

Sahina just smiled.

"Are they upset about our arrival? Do they wish us well or ill? Are we in danger here, on 186f?" Russell asked.

"The natives call this planet *Meraki*," Sahina said. "As for their attitude toward you…that will depend largely on you, I suspect. Life is always full of dangers. You will have to find your own way to self-discovery."

He nodded to them and looked off toward the forest, which was denser and deeper than it had seemed when they arrived, as spring season took hold of the land and the plants hastened to take advantage of the warmth and abundant moisture. He looked like he very much wanted to be moving along. But instead, he turned back to address them all, as if he had just remembered why he'd come.

"Try to be better humans than you have been. Understand, this is your last deliverance. This time, choose *life*. Choose the blessing."

Braelyn had joined them quietly, looking uncharacteristically timid. Keter then spoke directly to her, piercing her eyes with his gaze.

"What I mean is, don't fuck it up," he said.

With that, Sahina Keter turned and walked off toward the forest. He almost seemed to shimmer and fade out as he was leaving, but that was probably a trick of the light as the sun was just starting to set.

ACKNOWLEDGMENTS

I am truly grateful to the people who helped me bring this book to life. I confess that originally, I saw it mostly as a "bridge book," filling the function of bringing together its prequel, *Undue Influences*, and the science fiction series I am writing about the trials faced by a small group of humans trying to build a more worthy society on the distant planet Meraki. But as with all journeys, travelers have no choice but to mature along the way, and writing this book was a growth venture for me as well.

I found that undertaking a voyage that spanned light years across the galaxy inspired prodigious soul searching. We cannot, after all, travel such a long way in body or in mind without allowing for our spirit to adapt to and embrace its new reality. The questions of what it means to be human, to be a deserving human, and of how to maintain that noble state, demanded to be addressed, even if no clear answers were forthcoming.

To my beta readers, I am in your debt. Debbie Kurzban, who has been a huge source of encouragement throughout the creation of *Pillars*, lovingly labeled the places where the plot needed to be filled in as well as those elements that tickled her. And Sam Rafoss, for her insightful comments and appraisal, and who was essential in telling me that this book can, indeed, be read as a stand-alone novel.

To CB Samet and Isabella Adams, who took time out of their busy schedules to read and reflect, and to write such humbling endorsements for the back cover, thank you so much!

Thank you Dr. Christina Bellinger for your impromptu and valuable edits and for introducing me to the Vellum formatting program. That revolutionized everything!

Dorit Donoviel, PhD, Executive Director of the NASA-Funded Translational Research Institute for Space Health at Baylor College of Medicine, so generously allowed me to pick her brain on her extensive knowledge of the effects of outer space on human physiology and on pharmacology challenges. Only a fraction of what I learned from her is revealed in this story, but understanding that background helped me immeasurably in describing real-life effects of space travel.

My editors were superb. Carolyn Allard from Kirkus and Kemone Brown from THP Editing Service. I would use them again in a heartbeat. (i.e., for my next book!)

Cover design was created by Joe Montgomery, who is beyond amazing. For all his genius talent, he remains a skilled and unpretentious artist who follows through on all his promises.

To my friends, Ellen Gelerman and Fern Bernstein, who offered continuing support along the way, to Rabbi Todd Chizner, who was my sounding board as I developed symbolism for a brand new world, and to the myriad of Facebook friends who voted on cover designs, I am also quite grateful.

And, of course, I must acknowledge my two rescue cats who kept me in constant good company and to SammieKat in particular, who frequently stole my seat whenever I got up for a break. I am sure she did this to encourage me to sit still and focus for longer stretches.

Lastly, I would like to say a word of thanks to Mindy Kuhn at Warren Publishing. While she did not have hands on this book, what I learned from her in my past published works was vital to my ability to take on this project with the Very Indie Press.

ABOUT THE AUTHOR

Debra Blaine is a physician turned author. After thirty-plus years practicing medicine, she concluded that healing the spirit was even more important than healing the body. But how does one do that in our fractured society, where it is hard to encourage people to open their minds to other points of view? Her hope is that if she can get her readers emotionally involved in her characters, she may make more of a lasting impression, and perhaps some will think about the critical issues she raises from the safety of entertainment; simply hearing a story they might resonate with.

Blaine was born in New York City and grew up on Long Island, NY. She always had a passion for the humanities, and received her BA in the Plan II Honors Humanities Program at the University of Texas at Austin before attending Temple University for graduate studies in Comparative Religion. She ultimately changed paths, and matriculated at Baylor College of Medicine to earn her MD in 1987. She returned to New York for post-graduate training and practiced Family and Urgent Care medicine on Long Island and Queens for over thirty years.

She published her first novel in 2019 when she became

frustrated and disillusioned with the changing focus of the medical profession, which now closely follows a business model seeking to optimize profit even at the expense of sacrificing health. Her first book, *CODE BLUE: The Other End of the Stethoscope*, is a medical thriller that graphically exposes the effects of corporate greed on the American healthcare system within a fictitious plot involving serial murders.

As our culture in America has become increasingly polarized and extremism now passes for the norm, Blaine was inspired to write her second book, a political thriller titled *Undue Influences*. It postulates intentional, chemical brainwashing of the American population by the two political parties, and one man's struggle to resist and enlighten others, even while his life is being threatened.

Beyond the Pillars of Salt is the sequel, a dystopian fiction, which follows naturally from the events of *Undue Influences*. It is a representation of what our world might look like by the 2030's if we do not wake up and make fundamental changes. Not just to how we behave, but ultimately, to who we *are*. The warning in this novel is that if we do not learn to become better, more decent human beings, we will engineer our own extinction.

It is not essential to read these two novels in order, but doing so would fill in the back story in greater detail. The saga will continue as a science fiction series on the distant planet Meraki.

Blaine became a professional coach through FIA Coaching in order to help people shed their paradigms of what they think they "ought" to be and to reach for what will bring them joy and fulfillment. She is certified to train other coaches through this same organization.

In keeping with her new mission to present TRUTH IN FICTION, the Very Indie Press was established so that Blaine can format, platform, and distribute her books herself, cutting through the red tape of publishers who can take months to years. She uses top editors and cover designers and accepts nothing less than the highest quality. *Beyond the Pillars of Salt* is her first novel released through this venue, and having had the experience of creating a book from first word to publication, she now adds to her services the ability to coach writers at every stage.

Dr. Blaine loves animals, nature, and being outdoors. She has a grown son who is also a physician, and she lives with her two rescue cats in Suffolk County, Long Island.

There is more information on her website, at Debra Blaine.com or VeryIndiePress.com.

instagram.com/docdebwriter
facebook.com/DebraBlaineAuthor
twitter.com/debrablainemd